McARANDY WAS HANGED
ON THE GIBBET HIGH

Other books by Eleanor Berry

Tell Us a Sick One Jakey
Never Alone with Rex Malone
The Ruin of Jessie Cavendish (available in Russian)
Your Father Died on the Gallows (two editions, also translated
    into Russian and available in Russia)
Seamus O'Rafferty and Dr Blenkinsop
Alandra Varinia, Seed of Sarah
The House of the Mad Doctors
Jaxton the Silver Boy
Someone's Been Done Up Harley
O, Hitman, My Hitman!
The Scouring of Poor Little Maggie
The Revenge of Miss Rhoda Buckleshott
The Most Singular Adventures of Eddy Vernon
Take It Away, It's Red!
Stop the Car, Mr Becket! (formerly *The Rendon Boy to the Grave Is
    Gone*, available in Russian)
The Maniac in Room 14
Cap'n Bob and Me

Reviews

Tell Us a Sick One Jakey
'This book is quite repulsive!' Sir Michael Havers, Attorney
General

Never Alone with Rex Malone
'A ribald, ambitious black comedy, a story powerfully told.'
The Daily Mail

'I was absolutely flabbergasted when I read it!' Robert
Maxwell

The Ruin of Jessie Cavendish
'Eleanor Berry is to Literature what Hieronymous Bosch is to
Art. As with all Miss Berry's books, the reader has a burning
urge to turn the page.' *International Continental Review*

Your Father Died on the Gallows
'A unique display of black humour which somehow fails to
depress the reader.' Craig McLittle, *The Rugby Gazette*

Robert Maxwell as I Knew Him
'One of the most amusing books I have read for a long time.
Eleanor Berry is an original.' Elisa Seagrave, *The Literary
Review*

'Undoubtedly the most amusing book I have read all year.'
Julia Llewellyn Smith, *The Times*

'A comic masterpiece.' *The Times*

Seamus O'Rafferty and Dr Blenkinsop
'A riotous read from start to finish.' Ned McMurphy, *The
Dublin Times*

Alandra Varinia, Seed of Sarah
'Eleanor Berry manages to maintain her raw and haunting wit as much as ever.' Dwight C. Farr, *The Texas Chronicle*

The House of the Mad Doctors
'In this delightful caper, Eleanor Berry puts even A. J. Cronin in the shade.' Dr Joel Leskin, *The Stethoscope*

Jaxton the Silver Boy
'This time Eleanor Berry tries her versatile hand at politics. Her sparkling wit and the reader's desire to turn the page are still in evidence. Eleanor Berry is unique.' Don F. Saunderson, *The South London Review*

Someone's Been Done Up Harley
'In her tenth book, Eleanor Berry's dazzling wit hits the Harley Street scene yet again. Her extraordinary humour had me in stitches.' Thelma Masters, *The Oxford Voice*

O, Hitman, My Hitman!
'Eleanor Berry's volatile pen is at it again. This time, she takes her readers back to the humorously eccentric Harley Street community. She also introduces Romany gypsies and travelling circuses, a trait she has inherited from her self-confessed gypsy aunt, the late writer, Eleanor Smith, after whom she is named. Like Smith, Berry is an inimitable and delightfully natural writer.' Kev Gein, *Johannesburg Evening Sketch*

McArandy was Hanged on the Gibbet High
'We have here a potboiling, swashbuckling blockbuster, which is rich in adventure, intrigue, history, amorous episodes and black humour. The story Eleanor Berry tells is multi-coloured, multi-faceted and nothing short of fantastic.' Angel Z. Hogan, *The Daily Melbourne Times*

McARANDY WAS HANGED ON THE GIBBET HIGH

A Racy Black Comedy

Eleanor Berry

www.eleanorberry.net

Book Guild Publishing
Sussex, England

First published in Great Britain in 2005 by
The Book Guild Ltd,
25 High Street,
Lewes, East Sussex
BN7 2LU

Typesetting in Baskerville by
IML Typographers, Birkenhead, Merseyside

Printed in Great Britain by
CPI Bath

A catalogue record for this book is
available from The British Library

ISBN 1 85776 966 X

In memory of
Reginald Kray

It was a balmy June evening in eighteenth century London.

In an unlit Spitalfields backstreet, illuminated by a generous array of candles in a rough, noisy tavern, there was a dishevelled prostitute, known as Meg Parry. She was running backwards and forwards in a state of extraordinary excitement. The fact that she wore no shoes failed to deter her from stampeding along the sewer-stenched dirt track like an inmate of an asylum.

The backstreets of Spitalfields were not enviable places to live in. Some of them were only ten feet wide and punctuated by filthy alleys which were even narrower. The iron wheels of carriages frequently clattered over loose cobblestones night and day, making rest impossible, while refuse and human waste were thrown indiscriminately from windows.

Meg was shouting loudly and alternated her shouts with maniacal laughter. The sounds she made could have been interpreted as the baying of a tortured animal, or a crazed impoverished woman who had been proposed to by an aristocrat.

The thick smog made Meg too tired to run. She steadied herself by grabbing hold of a brick protruding from a crumbling wall a few feet away from the rowdy tavern. She stopped shouting and began to sing.

It would have been hard to describe her action as singing in the conventional sense. The noise she made was a strange, demented wail, a sound entirely out of control, due, not to its musical pitch, but to its very loudness. Bizarrely, the only thing commending it was the fact that her pitch was miraculously intact.

One might ask why Meg was behaving in this way. The explanation was simple. She adored an audience, without being particular as to what kind of audience, and she was prepared to wait for any audience, for nights on end if necessary.

As yet, Meg was only willing to sing the tune of her song

1

because she knew that the occupants of the tavern would soon spill into the polluted street, which was awash with discarded, rancid food, offal and sewage, so curious would they be to listen to her and look at her.

It was then that she planned to sing the words of her song instead of just the tune.

It wasn't long before the occupants came out of the tavern. Other prostitutes and their clients clambered down the steps, into the filthy street, swigging greedily from their cheap stone bottles of gin, as if they would never taste the beloved spirit again. They gathered round Meg and listened, fascinated, to her shrieking and singing.

Meg had always been an expert at attracting an audience and holding it interminably.

She backed away from them and pulled down the top of her dress, exposing her cleavage, almost to the point of showing her breasts, above which was a crudely-painted black dot.

Three men, who had emerged drunkenly from the tavern, called to her in unison.

'Go on, me doxy! Let's hear more of your singing.'

The audience made Meg feel she was about to faint with joy. She was under the impression that she held personal secret information, which enchanted and enthralled her. Although it was something sacred to her, she yearned to share it with others.

She had seen something earlier that day, a thing that had overwhelmed her with pleasure, a thing she wished to sing about to her assembled company, and a thing she revelled in because she had been avenged.

One of the three men started clapping.

'You're a nice-looking girl, aren't you, me doxy?' he said. 'We all want to hear what you're singing about.'

For a moment, Meg feared she would lose her audience. So desperate was she to describe what she had seen, that the deprivation of her audience would have broken her heart.

She flounced up and down the street and lifted her filthy dress and undergarments to show off her mud-spattered thighs. Suddenly, something broke within her. The feeling was like unexpected childbirth. She threw back her head and began to speak.

'Listen to this first, ladies and gentlemen. You don't know what I saw this morning!'

'Don't waste time. Tell us what you saw,' said one of the men who had spoken to her earlier.

Meg's appearance became even more seductive, regardless of her dirty rags. She looked sexually excited and leaned her head to one side, her smile showing two black teeth. She spoke in short breaths as if she had chest trouble.

'I got back from Tyburn just after dawn today and I saw a man 'ang,' she said in a voice scarcely above a whisper. 'The first 'anging I've ever seen in my life, it was. Let me tell you something. Lovemaking ain't nothing like watching someone swing, particularly when the bastard prisoner had killed your own sister. I don't want to be ribald, 'specially in front of them gentlemen 'ere, but an 'anging does something to a person, 'specially a woman. Begging your pardon for my coarseness, but you can feel the 'ole cursed lot gushing out of you, like some great waterfall when the noose tightens round the neck of the man who butchered and killed your sister. Now for my song.'

'For God's sake get on and sing it!' roared the puzzled audience.

What little there was of Meg's repetitive song cascaded from her mouth, her throat and even her tubercular lungs.

> *Jack McArandy was hanged at dawn.*
> *High stood the gibbet, O!*

She walked up and down the street, repeating the short song. Some members of her audience thought she was insane. But there were others who understood her, although some of them were irritated by her implication that she was unique in having attended a public execution.

In fact, most of her audience were Tyburn ghouls like herself. They, too, started singing about the notorious and deranged murderer, Jack McArandy, whose reputation they despised, and were comforted by the sweet revenge of the hangman's hand.

* * *

Jeremiah McArandy, a man of learning, was the first of that name. He was an orchestral conductor in the reign of William and Mary. His musical talent was exceptional, but his wife, Maria, was promiscuous and helped to destroy his mental state which, even at the beginning, was poor. Like her husband, she was musical and played the harpsichord.

Because of the suffering his illness entailed, his attendances to duty were erratic, and it was not long before that that he was relieved of his responsibilities. His health and his finances worsened when he became addicted to laudanum and he ended his life by shooting himself in the head with a pistol in 1702, just before Queen Anne ascended the throne.

Maria, Jeremiah's wife, had five sons, two of whom were illegitimate. The bastard sons, born five years apart, were called Edmund, conceived of a wheelwright, and William, whose natural father was an escaped convict. Maria met him in a London street and conceived William while being heaved by the convict against a wall.

William and Edmund died in infancy. Maria's remaining three sons, Henry, Joshua and Stephen, inherited Jeremiah's and Maria's musicianship. Because of their father's financial losses, they were raised in poverty in Spitalfields in a small cottage, the one thing the family could call their own.

All three inherited their father's insanity, but were able to earn what they could as wandering musicians. Henry and Joshua suffered from such severe melancholia that they ended their lives at different intervals and were survived by Stephen.

Despite his mental illness, Stephen had a tougher temperament than his brothers and was strengthened by his love for a seamstress called Sarah. She had long, wavy black hair and almond-shaped dark eyes. She was pretty, strong and resourceful, as well as being demure and endearingly modest. She caused him a degree of happiness by agreeing to marry him and keep house for him in the tiny cottage in Spitalfields which his mother had lived in.

Though living in reduced circumstances, Sarah came from a wealthy family in a more affluent part of Spitalfields and had grown up surrounded by servants, a series of governesses and a nanny to whom she was very attached. She was an only child. She was closer to her nanny than to her parents and it was her nanny's strong influence on her which enabled her to be spiritually strong and self-sufficient in later years.

Although Spitalfields was an area inhabited mainly by the poor, Joseph owned a grand house there, protected by spiked iron gates amidst a small cluster of similarly grand houses which stood out like diamond tiaras. Surrounding them, not too far away, were the damp, rat-infested hovels of those struggling to stay alive.

Joseph also owned a grand house in Buckinghamshire where he spent summers with his wife and daughter.

He had the makings of an astute and capable business-man. He owned a prestigious silk-weaving company in Spitalfields, where the silk-weaving businesses were based and the silk-weaving trade flourished.

It was the silk-weaving industry which gave Spitalfields its reputation in the eighteenth century as the centre of production of fine quality silks. The perpetrators of the flourishing silk-weaving industry were French Huguenot refugees who had settled in Spitalfields from approximately 1685 onwards.

However, discord and riots among the Spitalfields weavers were rampant. Mobs of weavers broke into buildings and cut into the looms of weavers working with more sophisticated machinery – one of the factors which ultimately occasioned Joseph's downfall.

As well as the silk-weaving companies, owned by the well-off, Spitalfields was equally known for the less fortunate who struggled as watch menders, tailors, carters, cobblers and bookbinders. Joseph inherited the company and two magnificent houses from his father, a non-drinking, clean-living workaholic.

Although he remained a dedicated and successful businessman for the formative years of Sarah's life, Joseph gradually became bored with his lifestyle and his boredom led to exhaustion and low spirits. He began to feel there was something more to life than being the owner of a silk-weaving company. All his life, he had wanted for nothing and he started to take his wealth for granted. Like many rich people, who did not spend their waking hours worrying about where the next penny would be coming from, he ceased to find money important.

To alleviate the monotony of his comfortable existence, he sought refuge in vice. He began to drink heavily and increased his intake of drink until he became an alcoholic.

He lost interest in his company, and did not even play a minimal part in checking its management and finances. His managers wrote to him, asking for an audience with him. They explained that they needed advice on the running of a captainless ship. They told him that discipline among the workforce had disintegrated to the point of anarchy, due to the boss's apparent abdication of responsibility.

He agreed to see the two anxious managers at his house in

Spitalfields at 10.30 one Monday morning, but forgot they were coming. The two managers arrived, bringing a letter written by Joseph, saying he was expecting them. One of his servants, an under-butler called Knight, admitted them to the house, perplexed and baffled. He escorted them to Joseph's bedroom, finding him alone.

The room was in darkness and Knight opened the blinds. Joseph was lying in bed on his back, purple-faced and red-eyed, clutching a three-quarters empty decanter of brandy.

'I hope you will excuse us, sir,' said Jenkins, one of the managers.

'Excuse you from what? Excuse you from whom?' replied Joseph, whose slurred speech was barely audible.

'We are the company managers, as you know. Our finances are dwindling because we have no direction. Our workforce is in total anarchy. Many of our men don't bother to come to work at all. Business was flourishing when you presided over the building once a day, calling meetings and giving us instructions. If we can't have your supporting authority, we will be ruined, sir.'

Joseph took another swig of brandy and stared vacantly into space.

Eventually, he said, 'I don't care if we are ruined. The business no longer interests me. Kindly leave my room. Can you not see I am drunk?'

The astonished managers left the room, each one making an inward decision to leave the crumbling company and set up an independent enterprise. Within a year the company became bankrupt and Joseph had to sell his Buckinghamshire house.

It was then that he realised the importance of money. He was determined to buy another country house and began to gamble. At first, he thought he had a flair for gambling and over the weeks won over two-thirds of the price of a grand country house. He threw his total gains on the tables and lost

7

them all. He spent the next few weeks trying to win back what he had lost and failed.

His wife, Cassandra, nagged him persistently and drove him to distraction. He turned to the pursuit of loose street women, to satisfy himself with the services Cassandra was denying him. Eventually he contracted syphilis which, in its tertiary phase, destroyed his brain.

He spent the last few years of his life lying on a bed of straw, soiled by his own waste, in an asylum overlooking a derelict part of Spitalfields. Cassandra had disowned him. On the day he died, just before his body was thrown uncoffined into an unmarked lime pit, deep cuts were noticed on his wrists and legs, just above his ankles. These had been caused by his desperate efforts to free himself of his fetters.

Sarah was only ten when he died. Cassandra was determined for her daughter to have a decent education. She knew that she would be alone in the world when she grew up and that without a background of culture and learning the only careers open to her would be those of a washerwoman or a prostitute.

Cassandra was by no means destitute. All she had lost were her house in Buckinghamshire and the family silver from the Spitalfields house. She was still able to employ Sarah's nanny and a governess.

She brutally chastised Sarah when her governess's reports were poor. Sometimes, she would whip her daughter, who was so determined to please her mother that she put a superhuman effort into her studies and became as well-educated as her governess.

She vowed to herself, spurred on by the memory of her father's fall from grace, to bring her own children up to be cultured and learn to speak educated English.

Despite the tragic circumstances ahead of her, she adhered vehemently to her vow. When she was 15, her mother died of a growth and the house in Spitalfields was in such a poor state of repair that it became unlivable in and unsellable, with no money available to restore it.

Sarah was completely alone and knocked on rich people's doors, asking if a children's governess was required. After a month in which she begged in the streets in order to survive, she found a kindly, rich family who needed a seamstress.

Sarah had met Stephen in a tavern and had caught his eye while he was playing the lute. Her black hair and almond-shaped eyes had appealed to him. They had introduced themselves and a short courtship had ensued.

At the early stages of their marriage, she had a calming effect on Stephen. She was modest, well-spoken and cultured. She was unwaveringly devoted to her husband. While he continued his work as a tavern musician, she remained in the employ of the rich family for whom she worked as a seamstress. She took work home and still managed to cook and clean for her husband.

After a few years of marriage, Sarah remained in good health and bore Stephen two sons, 18 months apart in age. As they grew they looked like twins, and inherited their mother's black wavy hair and dark, almond-shaped eyes.

It was Sarah who chose the names of her sons. Jack was the oldest and Ethelred was 18 months younger. The only physical difference between them was that Ethelred had a blond streak crossing the front of his hairline.

As soon as they were old enough to read, Sarah made a point of educating them for four hours a day, for the same reason her mother had supervised her education so rigidly. She hoped her sons would excel as men and possibly become clergymen or lawyers. Despite her fall from riches, she retained her educated brogue, and passed it on to her sons. They spent more time in her company than in that of their rough-spoken father and it was her accent they adopted and baffled others throughout their lives by their contrasting simple clothes.

Sarah taught them the fundamentals of English grammar, using the books she had kept from her childhood days. She taught them Latin, English history, geography, Greek history, algebra, scripture, English literature and even coaxed them into learning passages from Shakespeare for pleasure. To compensate for lost time, she worked at her sewing until the small hours of the morning.

* * *

One summer's day, Sarah was brushing the front wall of her cottage. She was the only woman in the street who did this. She was laughed at by her neighbours, but she was not self-conscious and didn't care what they thought of her as long as her house was clean and warm and her husband and sons were thriftily catered for.

Her sons were five and six years old that summer's day. They were sitting in the street just outside the cottage, bare-chested and wearing home-made cotton breeches. They were rolling a dice backwards and forwards at each other over the cobblestones.

The boys looked at their mother. Suddenly, they startled her by speaking in unison, as they were united by a bizarre, telepathic bond.

They said, 'We both love you, Mother. We love you more than anything in the world. Is Father coming home tonight?'

'He told me he would be. He has to earn his living.'

'What's that?' asked the boys.

'He goes round the taverns playing the violin and singing. Sometimes he takes his lute. Both instruments were given to him by Jeremiah before he became poor.'

'Will he teach us how to play?'

This time, it was only Jack who spoke.

The mother laid down her brush and put her arms round her sons.

'Yes, my boys. He'll teach you that. Two generations of McArandys have never lacked a musician.'

That night, Stephen did not come back. He had earned more than usual in the taverns and in the last one he visited he stayed behind after playing and got blind drunk. The next morning, he was in a foul temper and staggered home to Sarah who was again brushing the cottage wall.

'Where do you think you've been, Stephen McArandy? I have mouths to feed!' she shouted.

'Never you mind, woman! 'Tis lucky I came home at all.'

As he said this, a fit of insane rage descended on him, and he slapped Sarah across the face after throwing an abundance of coins on the table to show he had been working.

Though only five and six years old, the boys sprang from the cobblestones, their fists clenched.

'Don't you dare lay a hand on Mother!' they shouted.

The fact that they sprang up and spoke in unison, jolted Stephen. He went into the cottage, lay down on the Spartan bed he and Sarah shared and sunk into a dazed stupor.

Although Stephen was sometimes hot-tempered towards Sarah, due to his frequent heavy drinking after his evening's labours, he was gentler towards his sons. He taught them to play the violin and the lute and was impressed by their quickness to learn and their extraordinary display of talent, which surpassed his own.

By the ages of ten and eleven, they started to accompany him to the taverns and take it in turns to play the violin and the lute while he sang.

Despite their working alongside their father in the evenings, they did not love him because of his continued outbursts of temper towards their mother. They had always adored their mother, due to her warmth and unwavering kindness, as well as the feeling of security she provided, even when their father threw pots and pans at the walls when in a rage.

11

Ethelred and Jack taught themselves to be tough and resilient to protect their mother during these episodes. As she grew older, her physical strength and tenacity diminished and because her body grew weaker, so did her former lion-like spirit.

The boys began to resent their father because of the unpleasant atmosphere he generated in the home. Once, when particularly drunk, and the boys were aged 14 and 15, he came straight into the cottage, dragged his sleeping wife from the marital bed and violated her on the floor in front of the boys who were sleeping in the other bed in the room.

The experience sowed the seeds of a ruthless and frightening violence within the boys. Jack's violence and accompanying destructiveness were more extreme than those of Ethelred, but together they were becoming a daunting and formidable pair.

It took them ten minutes to register what was happening to their mother, as their knowledge of the facts of life was only rudimentary. As they grabbed hold of their father before pulling him off their mother, they made an identical movement, Jack holding his father's right shoulder and Ethelred his left shoulder. It was not the physical strength of his sons which terrified Stephen, but the manner in which their actions were performed in precise unison.

As they hauled him to an upright position, the boys punched him simultaneously on each side of the jaw. It was only their words which were not uttered in unison. Jack, the elder and fractionally stronger of the boys, spoke first.

'If you touch Mother again, we'll kill you,' he said in his educated voice.

The quietness of his voice and slow, deliberate manner of speech, as opposed to a shouted stream of invective, startled Stephen who turned to face Ethelred to gauge his reaction.

Ethelred was silent for a few seconds. Then he walked

slowly towards Stephen until he became so close to him that their faces were touching.

'I hope you heard what Jack said because he wasn't jesting,' he said.

For the next year, Stephen restrained himself. His sons, aged 15 and 16 no longer accompanied him to the taverns because their mother was becoming frailer still and they stayed at home to keep her company.

Stephen continued to come home drunk after entertaining. Without his sons to help him, his earnings diminished, as did his morale. Because of their reaction to his assault of Sarah, he crept into the cottage each night and crawled into the marital bed without waking her to use her fragile body.

His unnaturally moderate behaviour was short-lived. One night, he found his sons asleep and assumed that his demands on Sarah would go unnoticed. Without preamble, he forced himself on his unwilling wife until she screamed with pain.

The boys sprang from their bed, seized Stephen and dragged him outside into the deserted narrow street. Neither brother spoke. Jack seized Stephen from under the arms and banged his head repeatedly against the wall of the cottage, having pushed a handkerchief into his mouth to silence his screams.

While Jack continued to bang Stephen's head against the wall, Ethelred kicked him in the private parts and stomach.

The older man's body continued to show signs of life.

'Kill him, Ethelred!' said Jack in a hoarse whisper.

'A man can't murder his own father,' replied Ethelred.

The tone of his voice suggested he was unsure of his words.

Jack turned round and looked his brother in the eye, knowing that he had the power to hypnotise him and also knowing how much Ethelred respected and worshipped him as the dominant older brother.

The brothers pulled Stephen away from the wall and

pushed him to the ground. Ethelred continued to kick him in the stomach while Jack banged his head against the ground, battering him to death.

'We'll take him to the river,' said Jack.

Jack carried the upper part of Stephen's body and Ethelred carried his feet. Neither brother realised that Stephen's reasonably slim body would be so heavy.

It took them 20 minutes to reach the banks of the Thames. The brothers swung the body into the water. It covered a distance of about six feet. It was 11.30 p.m. and the tide was high.

Ethelred was nervous but Jack was unruffled. They watched the body sink and noticed the abundance of bubbles which were bodily gases rising to the surface of the water.

'But I thought he was already dead,' said Ethelred, his voice trembling.

'No,' said Jack. 'That isn't air. It's gas.'

'How do you know?'

'Because Father isn't the first person I've killed and thrown in the river.'

'How many have you killed?'

'Three,' said Jack abruptly.

It was about this time that Jack's attitude towards his naïve younger brother became protective, in the same way as his attitude towards his mother. He recognised that Ethelred, though violent like himself, was weaker than he and more vulnerable. He knew that with a degree of brotherly guidance, he could strengthen and toughen Ethelred and turn him into an identical replica of himself, whenever a crime had to be committed.

* * *

Neither brother spoke as they returned to the cottage. They

found Sarah asleep and decided to tell her about Stephen in the morning.

She woke to see her two sons dressed and sitting on her bed. Both wore black leather breeches, matching waistcoats and white shirts. They had made a point of washing themselves in a bowl from head to foot and changing their clothes out of respect for their mother.

Jack handed his mother a cup of sweet tea while Ethelred sat beside him in silence.

'I have tragic news for you, Mother,' said Jack.

Sarah was too exhausted to care. She knew her sons were unharmed and she felt safe. She raised herself with an effort, supporting herself with her elbows and stared first at Jack and then at Ethelred.

'It's about Father,' said Jack.

Sarah said nothing. She stared at Jack a second time. The right hand side of her face began to twitch which was something the boys had never seen before. They were reminded of the way in which she had aged before her time and were saddened.

'You tell Mother, Ethelred,' said Jack, to give his brother the sense of responsibility he thought he needed.

'Father had too much to drink last night, Mother,' said Ethelred. 'He left home late, after he startled you and made you scream. He went back to the tavern and had more. Then he went to the side of the river, I think to clear his head. He fell in and drowned.'

Sarah's face continued to twitch.

'How do you know?' she asked after a while.

'Jack and I followed him. We told him to come home. We followed him to the river. We tried to pull him away from the water but he struggled. We'd have lost our lives if we'd tried to go after him.'

Sarah sank back onto her pillow. Her face seemed younger. It had never been apparent to Ethelred and Jack how unhappy she had been living with her husband and how relieved she was by his demise. She did not have to communicate with her sons for they understood her and inwardly rejoiced with her.

'There'll be no funeral,' Jack said suddenly. 'We have not got enough money. Best to let him rest in the Thames. It's as good a grave as any.'

* * *

In the evenings, Ethelred and Jack made sure Sarah was comfortable and warm in her bed. Jack took Stephen's violin and Ethelred his lute to go to the taverns as their father before them. Their local tavern and the one they liked most, because of their popularity there, was called The Fife and Drum.

Because of their extreme musical talent, the brothers were also asked to play at weddings and banquets which were lucrative and enabled them to save considerable sums. Added to their comfortable earnings, they had enough stamina to walk long distances each day, aiming for more affluent areas than Spitalfields.

It was in these areas that they stole wallets from the pockets of men wealthier than themselves. They kept their takings among their honest earnings under the floorboards of their cottage, just in case they needed the money to help their mother. Before leaving, they locked the door and windows of the cottage to ensure no harm would come to her.

The brothers were more industrious in their trade than their father. They were more proficient as musicians and covered twice the amount of taverns their father had. They only drank in moderation once their evening's labours were over.

They were familiar with a large number of tunes and were almost always able to play whatever their customers requested after they had reached the end of their repertoire.

The Fife and Drum was so crowded with customers eager to hear their playing that many had to stand in the street. The McArandys had been entertaining until after midnight and their collection box was overflowing with coins. They smiled throughout their performance. With their black wavy hair and almond-shaped eyes, they looked, not like murderers but saints. They waited for the applause to die down.

'The night, alas, is no longer young. Have you a last request?' said Jack.

A wench-like, but pretty, blonde woman, with strange green eyes and a low-cut dress, and ringlets cascading over her shoulders, raised her arm.

'*Where have you been, Lord Rendal, my son?*'

'And that you shall have, my dear lady,' said Jack.

Neither Ethelred nor Jack had played this tune before but they played it perfectly by ear. Ethelred sang and played the lute while Jack played the violin.

The woman appeared overjoyed. She was also delighted by Jack's refined, educated accent. She made sure she would come to the same tavern every night in case the McArandys came there again.

Before returning home, Ethelred and Jack sat at a table and asked for some ale. They were satisfied by their evening's takings.

Jack was the first to speak.

'It's Mother's birthday next week. What shall we buy her?'

'We've made enough over the last few nights to buy her a piece of jewellery,' said Ethelred.

Jack inhaled on his clay pipe.

'I've never seen Mother in jewellery. I think silver would suit her more than gold. What do you think would be best – a necklace, a brooch, a bracelet or a silver and emerald ring? I feel only the best is good enough for her.'

'Emerald is a good stone for her,' said Ethelred. 'Do you remember that green silk dress that her mother gave her?'

'Yes.'

'A silver and emerald ring would go well with that, do you not think?'

There was a silence broken by Jack.

'What we've earned in the taverns and stolen wouldn't be enough for that,' he said.

'Then it's out of the question,' said Ethelred.

'On the contrary. There's nothing Mother deserves more with the dreadful life she's had. A silver and emerald ring it shall be.'

'How? We haven't enough money.'

'It's easy,' said Jack recklessly, 'we steal a couple of horses and rob a coach. That is if we don't get enough through pickpocketing.'

Ethelred was anxious not to appear weak in front of his brother, whom he feared on account of his insane streak.

'All right. You tell me what to do and I'll do it,' he said with extreme reluctance.

The brothers spent at least two hours discussing the possibility of highway robbery. Since they had lived in London all their lives, neither had any practical thoughts about stealing horses or finding their way to and from the country, or even finding a main road to London where highway robbery commonly took place.

They argued continuously about how best to obtain a silver and emerald green ring for their mother's birthday, or failing that, a piece of jewellery of equal worth.

It was Jack's rather than Ethelred's idea that they should spend half of their money accrued over the last years, as well as sizeable sums of money they had stolen on smart clothes.

They walked to St James's Street where they visited a tailor. By the time they had completed two fittings, they looked fit to be presented to kings.

The tailor they found was puzzled to see two scruffy men wishing to be transformed. Ethelred wore a ruffled peach-coloured silk suit. Jack wore a similarly patterned pale blue suit. Both brothers wore fashionably coiffed white wigs, secured at the back in a pony-tail by black ribbon tied in a bow.

The area they were in fascinated them because their mother had told them that that part of London had once been a mere collection of village-like houses, until the early eighteenth century, when it had been transformed by a significant growth of buildings, eating houses and shops.

They both felt ill at ease initially, as they walked from one opulent street to the next, but before long, a spirit of arrogance and confidence descended on them. They entered a small inn where they ordered a tankard of ale each to increase their courage, before they approached a busy thoroughfare, where a friend in the criminal fraternity had told them there was a jeweller's shop. They were told that it was 200 yards up the street on the left-hand side.

They walked up the thoroughfare in silence with their heads to the ground, the only feature of their appearance that would have struck an observant person as being odd.

Suddenly, Jack stopped abruptly and showed Ethelred a small jeweller's shop. By far the most attractive thing about the shop was the fact that it was manned by only one person, a middle-aged man who looked the worse for wear and who had a disinterested look about him as if he didn't care whether he sold his merchandise or not.

Jack rang a clanging gold bell. The shop-tender walked slowly towards the door and opened it. Ethelred stayed in the street out of sight, ready to crash into the shop at any given signal from his brother.

'How may I be of help to you, sir?' asked the shop-tender.

'Do you sell silver and emerald rings?' asked Jack.

'I am afraid I do not, sir. I sell diamond rings and ruby

rings. I take it the gift is for someone very special to you. Am I right, sir?'

'Yes. Would you mind showing me what is in the case?'

'Oh, indeed, yes.' The shop-tender picked up a diamond ring and a ruby ring and because his customer was so impeccably dressed, was foolish enough to lay the rings in the palm of his hand.

Jack seized the ruby ring and rushed to the door of the shop. It was a glass door with wooden panels. Jack threw his weight against it but found it was too stiff to open easily.

The shop-tender's reactions were slow. So astounded was he that his feet glued themselves to the floor. Jack continued to throw his weight against the door, until it crashed open and fell onto the pavement.

It was then that the shop-tender, a far fitter man than he looked, gathered his wits and chased Jack. As Jack was running into the street, he grabbed hold of Ethelred who was hiding in a doorway.

'Hold him, Ethelred,' he shouted.

Jack banged the shop-tender's head against the wall of the building while Ethelred held him.

Once he was unconscious, Jack slung him over his shoulder and whispered to Ethelred, 'I've got the ruby ring.'

Because the brothers were so immaculately dressed, the crowds, who continued to pass by, assumed that the shop-tender had been taken ill and that the door lying on the pavement had nothing to do with the episode.

As Ethelred walked down the street with Jack carrying the shop-tender on his shoulder, Jack shouted, 'It's all right. He's fainted.'

No one in the crowd took any notice.

Ethelred stayed by Jack's side. Jack increased his pace and broke into a run, continuing for about 20 yards. He suddenly swerved into an unoccupied alleyway, followed by Ethelred.

Both brothers looked furtively from left to right, to make

sure no one could see them. Satisfied, Jack dropped the shop-tender onto the ground to give the impression he had had an accident and turned to get away from the alleyway back to the street.

Suddenly, they realised he was conscious and as they were about to leave, they heard the feebly uttered words. 'I'll catch you. I never forget faces.'

Once more, the brothers turned furtively from right to left, to make sure there were no onlookers. They advanced slowly towards the shop-tender who was unable to get to his feet.

Ethelred sat astride him, throwing his whole weight onto him while Jack strangled him. The brothers coiled his body into a ball to give the impression he was asleep and turned the corner into another alleyway which was unoccupied, apart from a pile of rat-infested rubbish.

'Have you got the ring?' asked Ethelred.

Jack ran his gloved right hand over the palm of his left.

'It's all right. It's in the glove. Hurry up and change into your old clothes.'

The brothers took off their finery and neatly put their new clothes into the box the tailor had given them. From it, they pulled out their old clothes and Jack carefully put the ring in the pocket of his leather breeches.

Just as they had when they set out on their journey, the brothers walked home to their cottage in silence, apart from the exchange of a few words.

Telepathy between them was such that they did not always need conversation to communicate.

'Surely, you don't believe murder to be wrong, Ethelred?' said Jack.

'I don't really understand what it means, Jack. Sometimes you make me very confused. I don't believe in murdering those I love. You and Mother are the only ones I love.'

'Did you ever love Father?'

'No. I never loved Father,' said Ethelred. 'That is why I helped you to murder him. I also helped you because I knew it was what you wanted.'

The brothers were quiet entering the cottage for fear that their mother might be resting. They spoke in whispers.

'Where should we put the box, Jack?' asked Ethelred.

'Under our bed.'

'I hope Mother won't think the ring was stolen.'

'She'd be right, of course, but she'll love it.'

* * *

The following morning, Sarah woke a second time to find her sons sitting on her bed, and was relieved to see the expressions on their faces were suggestive of happier tidings than before.

As she opened her eyes, the boys held her by each hand.

'Happy birthday, dearest Mother,' they said in unison.

'Dear Ethelred! Dear Jack!' was all the mother could think of replying.

'We've got a present for you, Mother,' said Jack. 'You'll have to take it as it is. It isn't wrapped.'

Sarah fingered the priceless ruby ring in astonishment.

'This would have taken a few lifetime's wages,' she said.

'No, Mother,' said Jack. 'We earned it at one of the taverns in lieu of coins. The customer was a man of immense wealth.'

Sarah never doubted the word of either of her sons, whether she wished to or not. She had always forced herself to believe they were saints and continued to do so. She lay back and closed her eyes.

'Thank you so much, my sweetest boys,' she said and for the first time for several years she went back to sleep smiling.

The brothers withdrew silently from the room and stood in the street, leaning against the wall.

'It's a strange thought,' said Jack. 'I think nothing of

taking life. In fact, I enjoy it, but I'd be prepared to die for Mother.'

'After what you've taught me, I think I'd be prepared to die for you too,' replied Ethelred.

Jack took a while to answer.

'Yes. I actually think you would,' he said.

* * *

Some years had passed. Ethelred and Jack were 20 and 21. They felt in a nostalgic mood and returned to The Fife and Drum, where they had often earned so much money.

They were surprised to recognise the blonde woman who had requested *Where Have You Been, Lord Rendal, My Son?* They felt light-hearted and to humour her they played the song again.

It was then that Jack noticed her more closely. She had aged over the last few years, and her prominent green eyes bore a glint of cruelty and madness. This caused him to despise her because he recognised these traits in himself.

Accompanied by his disdain was a feeling of sudden lust. She waited for him until the end of the evening. He called to Ethelred,

'I'm staying the night here, Ethelred. You go home and look after Mother.'

'Staying here, are you? Who with?'

Jack pointed disrespectfully at the green-eyed woman.

'That one,' he said abruptly.

Jack took the girl upstairs, gripping her by the arm like a sack of potatoes. He had no wish to woo a street woman graciously, nor to bother using any primitive method of birth control available at the time.

Once upstairs, he started to undress and pushed the woman into an armchair. He made rudimentary conversation with her as he got into bed and pulled the sheet up to his shoulders.

23

'What's your name?' he asked.

She fidgeted in the chair as she was nervous. She found his black staring eyes as daunting as he found hers.

'Sally.'

'Any family?'

'My parents died of typhus. I have a sister called Meg who lives in Spitalfields with her friend, Liz.'

'Are they whores?' asked Jack, sounding like a cross-examining barrister.

'Yes,' said Sally, lowering her head.

She was as terrified of Jack as she was attracted to him.

'What about you? Are you also a whore?'

'Yes. My private parts are my victuals and drink.'

'You were here some years ago, weren't you? That was when you asked me to play *Where Have You Been, Lord Rendal, My Son?*.'

Sally remained seated. Jack thought she was going to remove her clothes but she didn't. A feeling of boldness suddenly took her over.

'I've been coming here every night for the last few years, because I thought sometime you'd be coming back,' she said, hoping to elicit some affection from him.

Jack caught her wild, shining green eyes once more. They made him despise her as well as himself.

'How sad that a woman should choose to waste her time in such a way, when she should be living respectably in a home of her own, bringing up a family,' he said.

She didn't answer. Nor did she cry. He noticed the hatred and hardness in her eyes.

'Take off your clothes and get into bed,' he commanded.

This jolted her so much that she failed to respond.

'Deaf, are you? Didn't you hear what I said? Perhaps you thought I didn't mean it.'

She was tired and wanted to go to sleep but she decided to obey him, so great had her fear of him become. He bit her savagely on the arm and scratched her chest before violating her, but his mood suddenly changed to gentleness and tenderness. He stroked her back and ran his hands through her hair.

'Nice lass. Nice lass,' he said.

His uncharacteristically kind words relaxed her and aroused her spontaneity.

'I had a dream since you was here last, all them years ago. I had the dream several times. That's why I wanted you to come back.'

'Tell the dream.'

'I was downstairs. There was them two big savage dogs. One of them was eating its way into the other. A fierce, frightening woman was whipping me, making me bleed. She was ordering me to pull the dogs apart but I couldn't do it. Then you came along, sir. You pulled her off me and set me free.'

Jack was bored. He knew Sally had an insane trait like himself and hated her for it.

'Oh, well, silly people have silly dreams,' he muttered. 'Now be gone. Perhaps my brother would like to give you a roll. He's more tolerant of whores than I am. By the way, do you have syphilis? I curse myself for not asking you earlier.'

'No, sir.'

'I hope not. I took the risk because I needed a woman badly, but if you were to give it to my brother, I'd seek you out and slit you up the middle.'

She stared through him with her hard green eyes.

'I assure you I'm clean, sir.'

'Then get dressed and be gone.'

She dressed and rushed towards the door. Once she felt she could leave the inn safely, she turned to Jack to tell him what she thought of him, in the light of his insulting and peculiar behaviour.

'You McArandys are insane!' she bellowed. 'You're both criminals, capable of cold-blooded murder, I shouldn't wonder. One day I'll have money. I'll have a horse and carriage. By God, I look forward to coming to Tyburn to watch you swing.'

She was already in the street by the time Jack got up and dressed to chase her. Had he caught up with her, he would have killed her.

* * *

As more time elapsed since the death of her husband, Sarah became stronger and more robust. Beforehand, she had spent the days in bed and her sons took it in turn to clean the cottage and prepare meals, which they had learnt to do when watching her before her health deteriorated.

Sometimes, when it was time to go to the taverns and she was not too tired after doing a reduced amount of the housework, the brothers took her to the taverns with them and enthralled her with their musicianship. She never stayed late, and either Ethelred or Jack took her home.

One evening, she told her sons she was too tired to go out and went to bed early.

The boys gave her an evening meal consisting of broth, beef, potatoes and gin before leaving the cottage.

'What was that green-eyed wench you had the other night like?' asked Ethelred suddenly, out of Sarah's eyeshot.

'She was fine enough once she frolicked, but there was something about her I didn't care for in the least. Her name's Sally.'

'What didn't you like?' asked Ethelred.

'I didn't care for her evil green eyes. Also, she's no more than a whore. So is her sister who shares a room with another whore. I personally would prefer a real lady, a woman of class, a woman who is not pert all the time and refrains from answering back when she is asked to do as she is told.'

Jack was walking faster than usual and Ethelred was getting out of breath.

'I think she's beautiful,' he said. 'Why don't we go back to the tavern where she always waits for us?'

Jack had not told his brother that he had threatened Sally with violence and assumed she would lack the courage to return to the same place. He had no wish to tell Ethelred that he had sunk so low as to threaten a woman. He felt sure that Sally would not be waiting, so he deceived his brother for the first time in his life and felt wretched because he had withheld information from someone he loved.

'All right, Ethelred,' he said. 'Let's go and find her for you,' adding with disguised sarcasm, 'and you shall see her in all her glory and maybe give her a good roll.'

To Jack's astonishment, Sally was in the tavern when the brothers arrived. She had only gone because she loved the music and knew she was safe surrounded by the large crowd.

Jack caught her eye and looked at her with disdain before picking up his violin. Ethelred smiled at her and bowed to her before kissing her hand.

'My brother, Jack, has already met you, I believe,' he began. 'I would like to congratulate you on your beauty.'

'Why, thank you, sir. Sally's my name. Perhaps I could be of some service to you at the end of the evening.'

Jack prodded Ethelred with his violin. He was impatient to start and was also becoming profoundly jealous of his brother for wooing another object of love and taking such an interest in what he considered to be a slut with evil green eyes.

Ethelred was unaware of the extremity of Jack's jealousy. Had he known about it, he would have excused himself from seeing Sally. At the end of the evening, Sally and Ethelred went upstairs to the same bedroom she had gone to with Jack. The bedroom had a red four-poster bed in the middle of the room and smelt of cheap scent, body odour and female genitalia.

27

Ethelred had never had a woman before. His approach to Sally was gentle and courtly. He took a while patiently removing her dress and corset. Then he carried her to bed and slowly removed his clothes before getting into bed with her. He had already taken the precaution of bringing a protective sheath, made of sheep's intestines.

She was surprised by the difference between the two practically identical brothers and felt puzzled when she noticed the blond streak near Ethelred's hairline.

'You're not at all like your brother,' she remarked in a pert voice.

'Ah, you are referring to my blond streak. Everyone downstairs has noticed that.'

As Sally had said nothing about Jack's brutal treatment of her, Ethelred still remained in ignorance of his brother's extreme physical hatred for her.

They lay on their backs for about ten minutes. Ethelred knew Sally was experienced and was seized by a savage attack of shyness.

'I must confess, I have never done this before, Sally. You'll show me what to do, won't you?'

'Aye. That I will. It's strange in a grown man, not to know what to do.'

She tried to stimulate all his erogenous zones. After a while, he was relieved of embarrassment as he felt ready.

He entered her, feeling he was a man at last, but suddenly the stiffness disappeared like the blowing out of a candle and he could feel the limpness, the humiliation and the shame.

He desperately wanted to prove himself a man and begged her for another chance. He was beginning to realise that he really preferred a man's world, a world in which he would never be separated from Jack. He also had a yearning to be taught how to please a woman for the sake of his personal pride and, what was even more singular, he had flashing fantasies of being spat at and abused by a woman.

'Please, Sally, give me another chance,' he said, a second time.

She failed to look him in the eye and put on her clothes.

'Perhaps, Ethelred. Perhaps not. You're a useless lover. I need a roof over my head which your earnings could rent. I don't have any feelings for you, but I can tell you have affection for me, which suggests you might like to rent me a room and visit me.'

'You're a hard, cruel woman, Sally, but I think I am in love with you,' he said, avoiding eye contact with her.

'If you want to know the truth,' said Sally, 'I like rough lovers like your brother, men who treat me like the whore I am instead of a pretence lady. He wasn't limp like you. He stampeded into my itching scut* and made me feel he was knifing me. You'd be surprised to hear how good it was.'

Ethelred almost cried when he heard of the manner in which the brother he worshipped had treated a woman. On the other hand, his love for him was so overpowering that he wished to imitate his technique which only a woman could show him.

He wanted to talk to Jack about it but was too ashamed of his weakness. After much tortured deliberation, he decided to rent a small room for Sally with his savings. He chose only to visit the room in the mornings so that he could spend plenty of time with Sarah and Jack.

* * *

Late one morning, Jack was waiting for Ethelred, standing outside his mother's cottage. It was almost as if he had become Jack's wife, so openly jealous did his older brother appear.

'Well, did you conquer the green-eyed whore?'

'I did,' lied Ethelred stiffly. 'What of it? She's only a

*Vagina: contemporary slang.

29

woman. I've decided I will rent a room for her to sleep in so that I can learn more tricks and woo other women. It's a necessary social grace. Don't be mistaken. I'll only see her for a couple of hours during the day. I'll come back to you and Mother after that.'

The brothers got into their shared bed. Unbeknown to each other, they both wept under the bedclothes. Jack wept because he had withheld information from his brother about threatening Sally with violence. Ethelred wept because he had lied to his brother about the alleged success of his lovemaking.

The McArandys continued to live closely to each other as before. Sarah remained healthy for a while, but had become too tired to accompany her sons to the taverns in the evenings, mainly because she found them hot and crowded and the atmosphere overpowering.

Ethelred agreed to Sally's request and rented a single room for her a few yards away from his mother's cottage. She remained unaware of the proximity of the room to the McArandys' home and would not have agreed to live there had she known that Jack was within walking distance from her.

Ethelred decided initially not to tell his brother that the room had already been rented, but he was unable to keep his secret for long.

'I see you're going out in the mornings,' Jack remarked one day as the brothers were having breakfast with their mother.

It would have been against Ethelred's conscience to lie to Jack because to him his brother was God.

'Yes. I told you before, Jack. I'm going to visit Sally.'

Jack turned abruptly towards his mother who was eating warm bread and honey.

'Would you excuse us, Mother? I want to take Ethelred outside to have a word with him in private.'

'So you're keeping something from your own mother, are you?'

Jack got up, went over to Ethelred's chair and pulled him to his feet.

'It's a matter of ribaldry, Mother. It wouldn't be right to talk about it in your hearing. We respect you too much for that.'

Jack led Ethelred outside, closed the door quietly and pinned him against the wall.

'What do you want with her, Ethelred?'

'Nothing, Jack. It's just lust, not love.'

'Then stop it. That woman can only cause you ruin and split us up. She could ruin us all.'

Ethelred failed to look his brother in the eye.

'I must see her, Jack. You wouldn't understand.'

'Indeed, I do not understand. Kindly give me an explanation.'

Ethelred decided to tell his brother the truth, although he would have felt less embarrassed had he lied.

'Oh, Jack, I'm no good with women! I don't feel as accomplished as someone like you,' he said, almost in tears. 'I need lessons.'

'Lessons? Lessons? What do you need to learn? You just get into bed and get on with it.'

Ethelred pulled aside.

'You and Mother come first, but you'll just have to accept my explanation.'

Before Jack could reply, Ethelred walked swiftly away towards Sally's room. He heard Jack's voice calling to him in the distance.

'If someone is capable of saying things like that to his own brother, he must love him more than he knows!' he shouted.

Once he reached the room, Ethelred found Sally lying naked on the mattress on the floor.

'Come, Ethelred,' she said, but he failed to notice the

mocking tone of her voice. He threw himself on top of her and entered her, managing to reach 20 strokes before he withdrew.

'That's a bit better, isn't it, Ethelred, dear?' she said.

* * *

For the next few weeks the incident helped him to perform fluently as a man. There were times when she was good-natured towards him and the occasions on which she had demeaned his incompetence had diminished. Sometimes she made him laugh, which endeared him most of all.

Without warning he realised he was uncontrollably in love with her and decided not to tell Jack, although this caused him torment and guilt.

Late one morning, he wandered back to the cottage and found Jack filling a bucket of water from a pump. Jack could not conceal his disillusionment with the fact that his younger brother, whom he thought he had created in his own image, should have allowed himself to be overshadowed by a woman of easy virtue, in contrast to Sarah's propriety and nobility of spirit.

'I see you're still flying back to that ageing street woman,' observed Jack.

'You don't understand, Jack. There's nothing serious about it. A man can be tough and still be allowed to shed his oats, can't he?'

'I have reason to suspect it's a little more than that,' said Jack. 'I'm not an idiot. Sometimes I see the expression on your face when you go out in the mornings. You look like a lovesick weakling.'

Jack's words hurt Ethelred, who had dedicated his life to copying his older brother.

He said, 'You're quite wrong. Sally is nothing to me. She's no more than a horse I care to ride for a bit of exercise.'

Before Jack could answer Ethelred walked out of his eyeshot.

'Going back again, are you?' called Jack.

'No. For once I am taking the liberty of going for a walk.'

Ethelred refrained from visiting Sally for two days. On the third day he looked forward to the abandoned frolics he would be having with the woman he had come to adore, irrespective of his words to his brother.

He kicked open the door of the rented room excitedly and strode forwards towards the mattress. Suddenly, he noticed Sally was not alone. She was lying on her back with her legs round a neatly dressed, muscular tradesman whose name was Christopher Ridgard. When Ridgard eased himself up and turned towards him, Ethelred noticed he was extremely handsome with blond hair tied in a pony-tail. Sitting in the straw in a corner of the room was a dishevelled street woman, swigging from a stone bottle of gin. She had long, tangled, dirty, blonde hair.

Ethelred thought of Jack and what he would have done in such a situation. Doing so gave him courage. He strode over to the mattress and dragged Ridgard off Sally. Then he kicked him in the stomach until he fell winded on the floor. He advanced towards the street woman in the corner, dragged her to her feet and slapped her face.

'Who are you and what are you doing in my room?'

Startled, the woman slumped back to the floor, unable to speak.

'I asked for your name, you untidy-looking slut,' he said, feeling Jack's spirit within him.

Eventually, the woman spoke.

'Meg Parry,' she said, her voice scarcely above a whisper. 'I'm Sally's sister. We didn't know the room belonged to you, sir. You don't come here every day and we use it for our trade.'

'Not without my permission, you don't. I want you and Sally's fancy fellow out now.'

By now Ridgard had staggered to his feet. Ethelred hit him twice on each side of the jaw, terrifying him, and threw him out. He then grabbed Meg by her filthy tangled hair, and was horrified to notice some of it coming out in his hand. He threw her out after Ridgard with such force that they collided on the cobblestones outside.

Sally lay on her back weeping. Although Ethelred still loved her, he was livid with her because of her betrayal, so much so that he was tempted to kill her.

'You've taken unfair advantage of me, Sally,' he said. 'I said you could stay here to keep out of the cold. I may not be a rich man but at least I have provided you with what little I have.'

She continued to lie down.

'It seems you have little of everything,' she said. 'Everything you own, everything on your person is little.'

He wrenched her to a standing position and shook her before giving an opinion of her.

'Everything about you is worthless. You are rotten to the core. As of now, you'll sleep on the streets. That is the door and your feet belong on the other side of it. Now get out!'

Sally put up no resistance and left.

As she did so, she put her tongue out at Ethelred, muttering, 'Always limp, always limp.'

At least Ethelred knew he had fulfilled Jack's wishes. He found Jack, once more at the pump, holding his bucket, singing *Where Have You Been, Lord Rendal, My Son?* under his breath.

'Hullo, Jack,' said Ethelred.

'You look happy today. Did you enjoy yourself?'

'It's finished, Jack,' said Ethelred, 'and I'm glad of it. She had a lover with her. I pulled him off her and beat him up. I threw them out and told her to sleep on the streets in future.'

A touching incident followed. Jack put down the bucket and hugged his brother.

'Welcome back to the McArandy fold,' he said. 'I'm proud to have you as a brother. I wasn't so proud of you before, but now you've become a man like me.'

He put his arm round Ethelred's shoulder and guided him into the cottage.

*   *   *

For the next few months the brothers and their mother lived contentedly. The friction between Ethelred and Jack had diminished, as had Jack's jealousy. The brothers continued to play music in the taverns at night and help their mother cook and clean the cottage during the day. Once the cooking and cleaning were finished, they sometimes played cards with her, to alleviate the boredom which began to descend on her as she grew frailer and older.

Sarah was not too weak to go to the market place each day. Apart from making purchases, she liked to gossip with other women.

She heard something one day which excited her and temporarily brought the colour back to her cheeks. She returned home with a smile. Her sons had been looking forward to her return and Jack took her heavy bundle of purchases from her and put it on the table.

'You look happy today, Mother,' he said.

'My sons, I have heard glorious news!'

'What news, Mother?'

'We have taken Quebec.'

'Who has? I don't understand.'

'The British have. General Wolfe led his men up a steep rocky hill, and surprised French soldiers when they were sleeping. Quebec's a British colony now. Give your poor old mother some gin and let her celebrate.'

Jack poured from the stone bottle of gin into a cup and handed it to his mother.

'So what year are we?' he asked.

'1760. You really ought to know that.'

'I'm sorry, Mother. No one can know everything. Where's Quebec, anyway?'

'Jack, dear, to think I broke my back educating you both! I'm astounded by your ignorance of geography. Ethelred, dear, fetch the rolled up map of the world from the drawer, and bring it here.'

'Of course, Mother.'

She unrolled it for her sons to see.

'Can one of you point to Quebec?'

'No, Mother,' said her sons in unison.

'Well, I must say, I am appalled by the ignorance of both of you. Look, it's here.'

'I don't understand why this is so important,' said Jack. 'Our enemies roam our streets. I wouldn't wish to attack a Frenchman. I've never even met one.'

'What is your poor mother going to do with you, Jack?' said Sarah.

* * *

The deterioration in Sarah's health came on very gradually. At first she grew tireder and went to bed an hour before she used to. She also began to sleep for two hours in the mornings.

Her sons noticed this change of habit, but were not overtly concerned until a few more weeks passed, when they noticed she was losing weight. They also noticed that the amount of sleep she needed no longer rested or relieved her. It was clear, from the groaning noise she made as she slept, that she was in more pain than she was prepared to admit to her sons.

Ethelred was woken in the middle of the night by her troubled sleeping. He rushed over to her.

'What is it, Mother?'

His voice woke Jack who went to his mother's bedside. Each brother knelt on the floor on either side of Sarah's bed.

'Feel this, Ethelred,' Sarah said in a hoarse whisper.

She guided his hand to her stomach and clasped it. Ethelred was horrified by the hard lump he felt which was the size of an egg.

'Now, you, Jack,' said Sarah. 'Put your hand on this.'

Jack did as he was told and muttered, 'Oh, Mother, oh, Mother!' as Ethelred, who was too horrified to speak, looked at his mother silently, shaking like a withered leaf, afraid of losing her.

'How long have you had it, Mother?' asked Jack.

Sarah turned onto her side to take the pressure off the area of pain.

'I noticed it a month ago. I had twinges of pain and didn't feel myself.'

Jack held his mother's hand.

'Take heart, Mother. It may not be too late to do something about it. You never know. A good surgeon might put it right. You may think it won't get better but I'm not prepared to give up hope. It's never been in my nature. What do you say, Ethelred?'

Ethelred managed to control his shaking, his courage returning due to his brother's words to his mother.

'He's right, Mother,' he said. 'We McArandys never say die.'

For the next few days, the brothers talked at length about how to raise money to pay for a surgeon before it was too late. The money they raised as musicians and thieves was far from adequate. They were taking it in turns to go to the taverns while one of them stayed at home with Sarah.

There was a man called Benjamin Stern at one of the

taverns. Stern was a highwayman and had always been a close friend to Ethelred and Jack. The three men often drank together after the brothers had finished their work.

That night, it was Jack's turn to work, and he happened to see Stern drinking ale at the end of the evening. As Jack approached one of the tables, Stern left his seat and came over to him.

'Good evening to you, Jack. Your playing was beautiful.'

'I'm glad, Benjamin,' said Jack, unintentionally shortly due to his worry about his mother's illness.

Stern assumed his abrupt tone was due to exhaustion and ignored it.

'Where's Ethelred this evening?' he asked.

A serving girl brought some ale over to the table. Jack and Stern drained their glasses in one go and asked for more. The ale relaxed Jack, and strengthened Stern.

'Oh, Benjamin, my family's in trouble,' said Jack. 'My mother's very ill with a lump in her stomach and we can't afford a surgeon. Our only hope is to turn to crime to raise the money.'

Stern leant across the table in Jack's direction so as not to be heard.

'You astonish me, Jack. The whole of London knows of the toughness and ruthlessness of the McArandys. Do you mean you are incapable of going out and plucking money from the trees?'

'I understand that but we've mellowed a bit,' said Jack. 'It's a long time since we last committed a crime.'

'Well, you can just de-mellow yourselves. I've done high-way robbery for twenty years. I live in relative luxury. I've never looked back.'

'How do you suggest Ethelred and I come by two horses? We keep pistols, but horses are something different. Besides, there was a time when we committed a serious crime in London. It's likely we weren't seen, but all the same, I think our next major crime should be in the country, nowhere near London.'

Stern looked exasperated.

'You steal the horses. Get out of London on a stagecoach. Find a well-to-do farm or mansion in the country. Break into the stables at the dead of night.'

'I'm used to committing crimes in London but I've never been to the country in my life,' said Jack in a bewildered tone.

Stern began to get impatient.

'I'll solve it for you,' he said. 'As I know your mother and she likes and trusts me, I will sit in with her tomorrow night. We'll say you are needed to play music together at a late night banquet a long way from home and will be spending the night out. You and Ethelred will get the stagecoach to somewhere in the country, not too far from London. Be prepared to walk a few miles. Find the two horses. Apart from that, all you need are masks to cover your faces. Then wait on the highway to London until a carriage owned by someone wealthy comes along and strip it bare. God knows, it's easy enough. It's my living.'

It was simple for Jack to explain the plan to Ethelred and to convince him that this was the only way to raise the money. Were Ethelred to refuse, it would have been his idea of committing high treason. To him, nothing would have been more reprobate or despicable than failing his mother and brother.

The theft of the two horses was easier than the brothers had envisaged. The stagecoach stopped near a town in Hertfordshire and as a fortunate coincidence there was a farm with several stables attached, two miles away. A publican in a local alehouse gave coherent instructions how to get to the farm. He believed Ethelred's and Jack's story that they had been hired as farmhands there and wished to sleep in one of the barns, to avoid having to get up at an unreasonable hour before reporting for duty.

It was 2.00 a.m. The brothers reached the farm, and were able to find the stables on hearing one of the horses neighing, sensing the intrusion of strangers. Both the brothers had had alcohol to steady their nerves. Jack was the first to open one of the stable doors, behind which stood a restless black stallion with a star between its eyes.

Jack took down its saddle and bridle. Although he had had no experience with horses in his life, necessity gave him initiative and it did not take him long to get the horse ready.

Ethelred found a chestnut mare in an adjoining stable. When it came to saddling and bridling her it was clear that he lacked Jack's intuition.

'Help me get it ready, Jack,' he said.

Jack tried to control his impatience. He went into the stable and got the mare ready, cursing his brother's incompetence.

'It's done now,' he said. 'I'm going back to my stable where my horse is ready. When I give a low whistle, that will be a signal for both of us to put on our masks and ride out of the stables. Close the door behind you. Do exactly as I say and don't do anything stupid.'

The brothers had remembered the whereabouts of the highway used by the stagecoach. They broke into a gallop until they got there. Then they stopped and waited.

* * *

It was 4.00 a.m. A gold and red carriage, bearing a family crest in lavish letters on its side was travelling along the highway. Ethelred and Jack rode onto the highway blocking its path. Had they been sober, they would not have been able to complete their mission.

The carriage, driven by four horses, swerved to a halt. Ethelred continued to wait in front of it to keep it still. Jack rammed the pistol he was carrying through the glass window and the light of the moon enabled him to see a man's and a woman's faces in silhouette. The woman was wearing a lot of jewellery, including a tiara. The man wore a series of rings over a pair of white gloves.

The woman was Lady Hockbridge, the sister of Richard Hetherington, the local squire who owned 15,000 acres of surrounding land. The man with her was her husband, Lord Hockbridge, the county magistrate. They were travelling to London, having been informed that their son had had a serious accident and had not had time to remove their jewellery.

Jack felt too tired and tense to bother to ask Lady Hockbridge to get out and divest herself of her jewellery, so he shot her at point blank range through the heart, reasoning that his mother's health was paramount.

Lord Hockbridge was too stunned to prevent Jack from ripping her jewellery from her body and putting it into a sack. Jack turned his horse round and rode to the front of the carriage where Ethelred was waiting. The coachman, whose name was Edward Hulton, was momentarily too shocked to react.

'Come on, go for it, Ethelred!' said Jack.

The brothers galloped off with the coach driver pursuing them. The chase continued for just over 200 yards with about 30 feet between the two horses and the coach. Suddenly, the mare Ethelred was riding fell and broke its leg. Jack brought his horse to a halt.

'Come on, Ethelred, get up alongside me,' he shouted.

Ethelred's action of mounting his brother's horse delayed their attempt to escape from the carriage drawn by four horses. While helping his brother up, Jack dropped the sack containing the jewellery.

Lord Hockbridge owned a pistol. He ordered Hulton to draw up alongside the brothers, now critically slowed down by the perilously strained single horse. Although horrified by his wife's murder, he had regained enough of his wits to point his pistol at the McArandys, whose masks had fallen off in the fracas. They pointed their pistols simultaneously at Lord Hockbridge. Jack shot him in the head and Ethelred in the chest, killing him instantly. They then aimed at Hulton, but Ethelred panicked and dropped his pistol and Jack's had run out of ammunition.

Edward Hulton had served in the Hockbridge family since the days when Lord Hockbridge's father was alive and was staunchly loyal to his murdered employers, who had treated him well and paid him generously, doubling his payment on occasions when they wished to travel late at night.

This increased his burning urge to pursue the brothers. Hulton was also known to Richard Hetherington, the landed squire who frequently dined at the Hockbridges' Queen Anne house.

Hulton had an exceptionally good memory for faces. He made a photostatic note of the maskless McArandys, whose horse had slowed down so much that it was now only ten feet ahead of the horse-drawn carriage chasing them.

For the first time in his life, it was Ethelred who took the initiative.

'Move off the road to the left and take us across that field,' he commanded. 'The carriage can't follow us there.'

Jack, who was holding the reins, and was still a little inebriated, wondered why he had not thought of this before. He wrenched the reins sharply to the left, hurting the horse's mouth and making it neigh.

Although the horse was exhausted and confused by being ridden by two strangers, the McArandys forced it to gallop for at least two miles through the fields, diverting their course from left to right at regular intervals, until it was impossible for Hulton to know of their whereabouts.

They were aware that they were on land owned by parties who could find them, once the news of the shooting had broken. They abandoned the horse and walked in search of a road, guided by the light of the moon.

They did not lie down to sleep that night but went on walking, waiting for the sun to rise. They were fortunate in that the sky was cloudless and the rising sun guided them just as the moon had done.

'We're not far north of London,' said Jack. 'We've no choice but to go there on foot. We'll be there if we walk thirty miles south. It will take us six hours. Can you do it?'

'Yes, I think I can.'

'You'll have no choice,' said Jack.

* * *

After they had walked for a further few hours through the fields, they found a dead rabbit lying on the ground. Just above it was a skeletal carcass wrapped in rags and rusty chains in an iron cage hanging from a tree. Neither brother spoke. Jack skinned the rabbit, scooped out its entrails and gave half of it to Ethelred. Although the rabbit was rancid and rotting, it was the best thing they had ever tasted in their lives and it gave them the strength to walk for the remainder of their long journey to London.

Just before they came into London, they found a dense wood to sleep in for a few hours. For the first time during their journey they were able to think clearly.

'We haven't been able to save Mother, have we?' said Ethelred. 'We've lost the booty.'

Jack got to his feet and wiped the twigs from his torn clothes.

'Don't give in. I trust Benjamin Stern. He's a good friend.

43

He'll know we've been in trouble and he'll stay with Mother. Once he realises we haven't been able to get the money, he'll find a surgeon for her. The only problem is she may not be curable. Don't get down-hearted. No one can say we didn't try.'

'But the Squire owning the land we were on and the posse of landowners accompanying him will get a description of us from that accursed coachman. They will all catch up with us, long before we get home to see if Mother is all right,' said Ethelred.

Jack picked up a stick from the ground and impatiently broke it against his thigh.

'I won't stand for this feeble, negative attitude. I know of dozens of safe lodgings and hideouts in London and I have contacts there. We stay at each of these for two to three nights at a time. We disguise our appearances beyond recognition and we get to Mother within a month. The search will be off by then.'

* * *

The first place the McArandys arrived at was a den of law-breakers in a broken-down building on a wharf by the river. Although the inhabitants of this place hardly knew Ethelred, they all knew Jack because they were familiar with his musicianship and admired his daring criminal pursuits, news of which had penetrated the London underworld. Three pipe-smoking burglars lived in the building, as well as four prostitutes and a pickpocket.

These people automatically assumed Ethelred was Jack's brother and gave them both a warm welcome and plied them with ale.

'What have you just done?' one of the burglars asked Jack as he sucked on his clay pipe.

Because his audience was so friendly and clearly supported

him in his endeavours, whether failed or otherwise, Jack told the truth.

'We tried highway robbery but we failed. Ethelred's horse fell under him, making it difficult to get away. A man in the coach pointed a pistol at us. It was either him or us so I shot him. The driver recognised us, so he'll spread the word and get the country squire and all the landowners onto us. We don't stand a chance.'

'You stand every chance,' said the burglar whose name was Tom. 'I suggest you shave your head and grow a beard. Ethelred, here's a red wig with a pony-tail. No one will recognise you in that.'

'Beards take a long time to grow,' said Jack.

'Then wear a false one.'

'Where am I meant to get that?'

Tom whistled as if to a dog.

'Freddie, come over here.'

The man addressed as Freddie did so. Tom leant forwards and wrenched off the false blond beard he had been wearing for a month. An equal growth of beard was hidden underneath it.

'Now for something which sticks,' said Tom.

Freddie produced a sticky substance from his pocket and passed it to Jack who took the beard from the burglar.

'You don't mind, Freddie, do you?' asked Jack.

'No, lad. You've given me so much pleasure from your musicianship, it's the least I can do in return.'

The McArandys stayed with their friends for another two days. Now that Ethelred was wearing his wig and Jack had shaved his head and was wearing a blond beard, it was impossible to recognise either of them.

Once they had left their friends, they moved on to an alehouse where they knew they would not be recognised. They were tired and under stress because of their mother, and were relieved to be regarded as strangers and not to have to make cheerful conversation. They made a point of sitting at separate tables and refrained even from looking at each other.

They moved from one hiding place to the next for a month. By this time they were terrified that they would arrive too late to find their mother alive. They wondered how long Benjamin Stern would be prepared to wait for their return before assuming they were dead.

Since the visitors to The Fife and Drum, were all in the criminal fraternity, as well as being devoted to the brothers, they were not afraid to go back there and joke about their disguises. They accounted for their adventures in the country, drew further attention to their new looks and had their companions in paroxysm of laughter.

*   *   *

The spirit of merriment did not last long. The McArandys became drenched in gloom because they knew they were about to return to their mother. Even Jack was afraid to make enquiries about her, but after drinking two tankards of ale he summoned the courage to ask his friend of many years, Jeff Gordon.

'As you know, I've been away a while, Jeff. Have you seen or heard anything of my mother?'

Gordon gave him a strange side-ways look as if hiding something which he thought would frighten Jack. He drank more ale.

'Your mother, Jack? Why, I've seen nothing of her since long before you went away. I was given to understand she'd been taken a bit poorly. Well, it was you who said that, in fact. Have you been home since you came back?'

'No,' said Jack in a hoarse whisper.

Gordon slapped him on the back.

'If anything had gone wrong, surely we'd all know. We think highly of her in here. She's a fine lady.'

Jack looked at the floor in despair, fractionally comforted by the ale. Then he called to Ethelred.

'I'm afraid it's time to go home now. Have you had enough ale?'

'Yes, but it's a vile business.'

'Even so, we've got to get on with it,' said Jack.

The brothers walked from the tavern to the cottage, their heads bowed. They threw open the door, causing it to bang against a wall.

'Be strong, Ethelred,' said Jack. 'There's a good lad.'

The McArandys walked slowly towards Sarah's bed. Her hair was combed and she was lying on her stomach under the bedclothes as if serenely asleep.

Ethelred felt a surge of joy. It occurred to him that Benjamin Stern had been looking after her during his long absence and that he had arranged for a physician to give her laudanum to ease her pain.

'Let's turn her over, just to make sure she's breathing all right,' said Ethelred.

The brothers turned her gently as if she were a piece of Dresden china.

The first thing they saw was her face. Her cheeks, chin and forehead were almost unlined like a little girl's.

Her eyes had been savagely gouged out.

While Jack ran to the table to take a few swigs of gin, Ethelred ran behind his mother's bed to be sick. As he rose from a stooping position, he saw something else which was obscured in the semi darkness.

Stern was lying on his stomach with a knife in his back buried to the hilt. In the dust on the floor by his side were written the letters GR. It was not possible to know whether these letters formed part of a word or whether they were someone's initials. Jack bent over to scrutinise them before forcing himself to his feet. He and Ethelred stood motionless for a few minutes with their arms round each other's waists and for the first time in their lives they wept.

Jack was the first to break the silence.

'There's some gin left, Ethelred. Let's finish it to clear our heads. Then we'll know what to do.'

The brothers poured the gin into two cups, allowing themselves half each. Although they felt nauseated because of the amount of ale they had consumed, their nerves became calmer, Jack's more so than Ethelred's, who paced up and down the room, shouting.

'What are we to do, Jack? How can we call anyone out here when the law's already after us? How can we arrange for Mother to be given a proper burial when the first question that's going to be asked, is why have her eyes been gouged out? They're going to think we did it, aren't they?'

Jack realised that the only way to deal with Ethelred was to slap his face. The slap brought him to his senses.

'Calm down, you fool! Are you a McArandy for nothing? In the circumstances, there's only one way out. We can't do anything about Benjamin and I'm afraid we cannot give Mother a burial.

'It's not yet dark. We have no choice but to burn the cottage down. We can't do that until after dark. We're in luck because the four tall candles on the table are still burning.'

'What do I do?' asked Ethelred, who was too intoxicated to think.

Jack lost his temper.

'You really are absolutely half-witted! What do you think you do once we've got a fire going and we want to burn down a cottage?'

Ethelred was still stunned and his wits were not about him.

Eventually, he said, 'I'll find all the music sheets in the drawers and break up the chairs and add them to the fire.'

'Correct. At least we've been keeping our musical instruments in The Fife and Drum, where we've been picking them up before playing in the other taverns, and taking them back there as our last, stopping place.'

They waited until the early hours of the morning. Jack used one of the candles to set alight the bundle of tinders his mother had kept by the fire. The tinders were brittle and dry. A flame, larger than expected, leapt into the air. As Jack fanned it with one of the music sheets, Ethelred poured more sheets onto it, sweeping the fire towards the wooden walls, the spartan beds and the table which Sarah used to work at as a seamstress.

It took ten minutes for the cottage to be completely ablaze. Ethelred and Jack stood by the door and waited for the bodies to be consumed before rushing out into the night and making their way to the lodgings by the wharf. The law-breakers there had been kind to them and would no doubt be pleased to accept rent from them.

* * *

The time was 2.00 a.m. when the McArandys banged on the wall of the lodgings. It was Freddie who opened the door for them, alarmed because he and his friends lived in fear of arrest.

'You gave me a fright, you did, you terrible McArandys! What's the matter?'

'Our little cottage has been burnt down and everything in it,' said Jack, who decided not to say anything about Stern and Sarah.

'I'm sorry. You poor, poor lads! Come in and I'll have some sausages heated for you.'

Once seated on the floor, since the only table was covered with knives, axes and cudgels, Jack mentioned the rent.

'We've saved enough to pay you rent,' he said. 'Is it all right if we stay here for a while?'

Freddie spat out part of his sausage because the meat was rotten.

'You can stay here for ever as long as you pay rent,' he said. 'Sixpence a week will suit us nicely.'

The McArandys were shown to two hammocks in the same room they had eaten in. It was not until the next morning that they left the building to discuss plans to find the murderer with the initials GR.

They decided they would wait at least six months to do this and reasoned that the search for them after their adventures in Hertfordshire, had diminished, if not considerably died down. They resumed their natural appearances, as although they were not fanatical chasers of women, it appealed to their vanity to know that women looked at them and lusted after them.

*　　*　　*

The first tavern the McArandys went to after their mother's death was The Fife and Drum, the one they played in more frequently than most and which was closest to their burnt-down cottage. They approached their friend, Jeff Gordon.

'We're looking for someone with the initials GR. Do you know anyone with those initials?' asked Jack.

Gordon shifted his weight from one foot to the other. Earlier that night, he had burgled a house and had only just managed to get away without being detected. He was still feeling shaky and shocked.

'GR,' he said. 'Does he live near here?'

'Yes, I think he does.'

'The only man I know with the initials GR is George Robertson, a mean Scotsman. I played cards with him once in The Black Boy Inn round the corner. A filthy cheat he is. I won't be playing with him again.'

Ethelred jolted himself out of his silence and entered the conversation for the first time, extending the index finger of his right hand.

'Oh, he cheats at cards, does he?'

'Yes,' said Gordon. 'When I told him he was cheating, he overturned the table and challenged me to fight him.'

'Did you fight?'

'It wasn't a proper fight. He punched me in the jaw, and knocked me down. Then he disappeared into the night.

Jack asked, 'Before you started your game, did he say where he lived or how he earned his living?'

'Yes. He seemed friendly at first. He said he was a carter by trade. He lives with his father in Tinley Street.'

'Is his father also in trade?'

'No. He doesn't work now. They say his health is bad. He's getting over typhoid, I think. Robertson cooks breakfast and supper for him.'

'Where is Tinley Street? I've never heard of it,' said Ethelred.

'Strange you don't know where Tinley Street is. Come outside with me. It's quite near here. I'll show you.'

'Thank you, Jeff,' said the brothers simultaneously.

Jeff had never heard them speak in unison before and was startled.

It was raining hard but the three men stood in the street oblivious of the rain.

Gordon said, 'Go left and walk on for about a mile until you come to a church on the other side of the street. Cross over. Go past the church, turn right, right again and first left. The second turning left after that is Tinley Street. It's a very small street but I don't know which house it is.'

'What does Robertson look like?' asked Ethelred.

'He's easy to recognise. He's six foot tall. He has long red hair and a thick red beard and speaks with a strange nasal accent. He told me he left home at 7.30 every morning.'

* * *

Tinley Street was hovel-ridden, untidy and filthy. Rat-infested rubbish, months old, littered the sides of the street. The brothers assumed that the filth had contributed to a recent typhoid epidemic. The cobblestones were loose and many of them missing as if the street were subject to riots. The tiny houses were damp and dirty with cracks in their doors and walls.

Even without sufficient evidence, the McArandys convinced themselves and each other that Robertson was the murderer of their mother and Stern and that the initials written in the dust were his.

They hid behind a pile of foul-smelling rubbish, and waited until the following morning in the pouring rain. Due to the street's filthy conditions, its inhabitants were struck by one typhoid epidemic after another, and most of the inhabitants of the neighbouring streets were also ridden with the disease.

* * *

Robertson had overslept and left his dilapidated-looking house at 8.00 a.m. His red hair and beard made him immediately recognisable. He was carrying a loaf of bread under his arm to eat for his lunch and his gait was hurried and agitated. He rushed past the pile of rubbish hiding the McArandys, who leapt over the pile and threw themselves onto him, bringing him to the ground. Both brothers lay on top of him.

'What is this?' gasped Robertson.

Jack banged his head on the cobblestones, causing his forehead to bleed. The brothers wrenched him to his feet and gripped him by the arms. He dropped his loaf of bread onto the ground and swore to himself.

'We know you. Your name's George Robertson. You cheat at cards, don't you?' said Ethelred. 'We also heard that you are violent.'

'I don't know what you're talking about. Leave me alone,' said Robertson in a hoarse whisper.

'It's not really that we've come to talk to you about,' said Jack. 'You're to come with us. There's something we want to show you.'

'There's no need to hold me so tight. I'll come with you, but I don't know what I have ever done to either of you.'

Jack kicked him in the stomach, winding him while Ethelred held him still.

Jack said, 'You say you don't know what you did to either of us, but we're going to show you what you did to both of us.'

'Please. Let me go. I don't know anything,' said Robertson.

The brothers ignored him. They marched him in silence to the site of the burnt-down cottage over a mile away from Tinley Street. They pushed him to the ground and buried his face in the ash-covered earth where the cottage had been and wrenched him to his feet.

'You came here one night, didn't you?' said Jack.

'I've never been here! I've never been here!'

'Yes, you have. A cottage stood here once. You broke in and found a sick old lady lying in her bed and a man looking after her because she was alone.'

'I never broke in. I never saw anyone!'

'You lie! You lie! You lie! You lie! You dug out that poor old lady's eyes, and because there was a witness, you killed him too. You could have got away with your crime but you made one mistake. For some reason, you wanted to leave your mark to gratify your vanity. You wrote your initials in the dust on the floor by the man's body. We know why you did it, too. You did it because you knew about us and you couldn't kill us so you decided to break our nerve. That lady you killed was our mother. You worked your murder out in advance, didn't you?'

'No! No!'

'All right,' said Jack, 'we'll make an agreement with you. If you confess, we'll let you go. In other words, we'll forgive you.'

'I didn't do it.'

'Your initials are GR, are they not?'

'Yes, but so are a lot of other people's.'

'Not in this neighbourhood, they're not. You may live round here, but you speak with a strange and horrible accent. You don't come from London, do you?'

'No. I am Scottish but I've lived here all my life.'

'We're just as tired of this as you are,' said Jack. 'Just say "I killed your mother" and we'll let you go.'

Robertson had the impression that the brothers were not hardened criminals but concluded they were mentally unstable. He had been reprimanded for being late for work on several occasions and had been threatened with dismissal. He decided to trust Jack's word and make a false confession. He had been brutalised enough and felt too weak to care about his honour.

He said, 'I'll agree to say whatever you want as long as you both let go of me.'

'Well, what have you to say?' said Jack. 'Tell the truth and we'll let you go.'

Robertson sank to his knees as if receiving benediction.

'I confess to the murder of your mother and to the murder of the man guarding her. My initials are GR, standing for my name which is George Robertson and I wrote them in the dust by the body of the man I killed. I know it will not be easy, but I hope you will see fit to forgive me and let me go as you promised.'

Jack kicked him in the stomach a second time. As Robertson lay on the ground, his spirit completely broken, Jack bent over him and mimicked his heavy Scottish accent.

'You fool for believing me and thinking I'd keep my word! Hold him, Ethelred, while I finish him.'

Ethelred did as he was told. He sat astride Robertson while Jack kicked him repeatedly on the head until there were no signs of life in him.

Neighbours tended to turn blind eyes whenever the McArandys committed crimes in broad daylight, partly because they were terrified of them and partly because they respected and adulated them as folk heroes and musicians who gave inordinate pleasure.

Just as they had their violent father, the brothers carried Robertson's body to the banks of the Thames and swung it into the water.

As the brothers were walking away from the river, to their lodgings by the wharf, Jack, who was overtly sensitive to moods in others, suddenly noticed that Ethelred was depressed. He put his hand on his shoulder.

'What's the matter, Ethelred? Why are you so down in spirits?'

Ethelred put his arms behind his back and stared at the ground.

'After thinking about it, I don't think the man we threw in the river was the same man who killed Mother, just because his initials were GR.'

'But he confessed to murdering her. Weren't you listening?'

'He only confessed because we were bullying and bludgeoning him.'

Jack thought a while. He also concluded that just because the man's initials were GR it didn't necessarily mean he was the murderer. It was not a pleasant thought so he forced it out of his mind.

'Don't get so moral all the time, Ethelred. He didn't seem a very nice man. What gentleman plays cards for money and cheats? What gentleman punches his opponent in the jaw when the opponent has the courage to say he's cheating? It shows he was given to violence.'

'Well, what about us?' asked Ethelred.

'Ours is a different sort of violence. We commit it, with the odd exception, to do good, like to steal a ring for Mother's birthday, to resort to killing on the highway to raise money to pay for her to see a surgeon. I'm not saying we're saints but we do on the whole abide by a moral code of sorts.

'It just chanced that we found a man whose initials were GR and that man had had a violent and cheating reputation. Robbing a stagecoach is one thing but cheating at cards is deplorable.'

'Why?'

'Because when you're sitting at a card-table your companions assume you are a gentleman. When you're committing highway robbery you are automatically seen as a scoundrel. Besides, with Robertson we needed a scapegoat. The anger and bitterness about Mother is still burning so much inside both of us that I'd be prepared to do the same to anyone with the initials GR, just to eliminate the lot of them. I'm sure you would too.'

Ethelred sat down on a low stone wall. Jack remained standing.

'Are you telling me that you want us to track down people with the initials GR for the rest of our lives when we're not working and not do anything else?'

'Not all the time, Ethelred. Only some of the time. We ask casually here and there, size the man up and if he's wicked, we give him the same treatment.'

'What do we do if this man with the initials GR, who really killed Mother, has left the neighbourhood? He may have left London altogether. He may have gone overseas.'

'I'm finding him, Ethelred and you're going to help me.'

'Isn't it going to look very suspicious if all the corpses found in the river have the initials GR?'

'What should this have to do with us? I'm going to do the rounds of taverns frequented by criminals, places I'm known and respected in. I hope you'll help me.'

'I'll always help you, Jack.'

'Good lad, I'm sure you will,' said his brother.

*   *   *

The McArandys decided to take the following night off. They went to an inn where they were known only vaguely as being musicians and not as criminals. The floor of the dining area of the inn was covered in sawdust and the tables, which were round and bare, occupied the centre of the floor. Customers were allowed a full dinner or drinks alone if they preferred.

Ethelred and Jack sat down at a table and were brought a tankard of ale each. Suddenly Jack's attention wandered. At a neighbouring table sat a woman of about 20, recently widowed. She was dressed elegantly in black, which accentuated her natural-looking unpowdered blonde hair in neat ringlets and her general mien of humility and modesty.

Jack was immediately struck by her delicate, fair skin, her honest blue eyes and her petite profile. He noticed she had tears in her eyes.

'Sorry, Ethelred. I'm going to have to leave you alone. For the first time in my life, I've fallen in love.'

Ethelred never thought that would happen to Jack. He said nothing and looked aghast.

Jack walked discreetly over to the woman. She was attracted by his good looks. He looked her in the eye and smiled.

'Good evening, madam.'

The woman batted her eyelids and lowered her head shyly.

'Good evening, sir,' she said quietly, but with a semblance of a smile which delighted Jack.

'Would you like me to join you, or would you rather be alone? I shan't think it rude if you say you wish to be alone.'

The woman brushed away a tear on her cheek. She would have given anything for company that evening. Though wealthy, she did not feel the urge to dine in pomp, which is why she chose the humble inn.

'I would love to dine with you, sir,' she said graciously.

'Good,' said Jack. 'I congratulate you on having made the right decision.'

He gave her a charming smile.

'I think I did make the right decision, sir.'

'No. Not sir. Jack McArandy's my name. Just call me Jack. What's your name?'

'Priscilla.'

'That's a pretty name, as pretty as its owner. I expect you're hungry.'

'I am. I haven't eaten since this morning?'

'Why, if I might ask?'

'I had to see my hairdresser.'

'Your hairdresser has made your hair look lovely.

'Thank you. I like it to look natural. I detest powdered hair.'

The serving lady was wench-like and sullen. She knew who Jack was and kept staring at him. She brought gin, soup and beef to the table. Priscilla was the first to break the silence.

'You did say your name was Jack McArandy, did you not?'

'Yes, I did.'

'I've heard of you. You and your brother are famous musicians. What is your brother's first name?'

'Ethelred. He's the man sitting over there.'

'You look very alike. Are you twins?'

'Not twins. Brothers. Everyone thinks we are twins. There are eighteen months between us.'

'I would love to come and hear you play.'

Jack was evasive. He was uneasy about the rich, probably respectable woman, visiting The Fife and Drum which was frequented mainly by law-breakers.

He said, 'Perhaps we'll come here one evening, provided you come as well.'

She didn't answer but nodded at him and smiled.

'You must understand, Priscilla, I am not a rich man. Ethelred and I live only on our earnings. Sometimes we earn a great deal. Other times, we are less fortunate. We earn enough to live well and enjoy life but that is all. Perhaps a wealthier man would suit your needs better than myself.'

'I do not seek wealth in a man, only love. My husband left me a lot of money so I am not wanting.'

As she spoke, Jack noticed a tear on her cheek and wiped it off with his finger.

'Did you love your husband?'

'Yes, but I am recovering from my grief. I am afraid we had no children.'

*   *   *

Priscilla was the only child of Arthur and Isabella Ashley. Her father was wealthy and had counted on having a son. His wife gave birth to two stillborn daughters, three and four years after Priscilla was born.

Both the Ashleys were austere and domineering parents and from the age of ten onwards they impressed on Priscilla the importance of eventually marrying a rich husband whom they said they would choose themselves.

Because of her lonely and repressed childhood, Priscilla was a demure. solitary, withdrawn girl of little self-esteem. She had minimal contact with her parents except at meals which were eaten in silence. She was intelligent and hard-working and gained her education from a strict, critical governess who gave her the impression that she was academically backward.

Priscilla was determined to reach the standards imposed on her and by the age of 15 she had become studious of her own volition and dedicated her lonely life to improving her mind to satisfy the husband whom her parents would choose for her.

She was afflicted by intermittent attacks of melancholia, which were diminished to some extent by Mrs Dodderidge, her loving nanny. These baffled and shamed her so she suffered them in silence and waited patiently for them to pass. In order to combat them, she sat in her room reading improving books.

Novels did not help her, however, since many of the characters in them suffered from negative thoughts and self-doubt which she found infectious. Instead, she read books about history, which made no emotional demands on her and took her out of herself.

When she was tired of reading, she gained some pleasure and emotional peace of mind doing tapestry. The rhythmical sewing movements of her hand were therapeutic and sent her into a kind of trance which sometimes blocked the melancholia's descent on her shy, fragile psyche.

Added to this hobby, she became vain. She had felt unloved because her father continually impressed on her his regret that she had not been born a male and because she felt her intensive reading was not making her any cleverer. She realised, however, that she was uncommonly pretty with her flowing golden hair like sheaves of corn, her big blue eyes, pert, straight nose and her double-bowed mouth.

It delighted her when her mother sent for the dressmaker to fit dresses of every colour onto her slender figure and it cheered her to spend long periods of time gazing at her reflection in the full length mirror in her room.

Unlike other vain, young women, Priscilla's vanity was unaccompanied by precocity of spirit or conceit. She remained shy, modest and self- effacing, despite her beauty.

Priscilla met her husband-to-be at a ball in London, hosted by a friend of her parents. His name was Rupert Medcalf. He was about six foot tall, with a thick mane of blond hair like her own. As soon as they were introduced, they were mutually attracted.

Unbeknown to Priscilla, her parents knew Medcalf wished their daughter to marry him. She feared they would oppose her choice of suitor and forbid them from meeting again. What she did not know was that Medcalf was a man of immense wealth and that he hid his wealth from others so that they would not befriend him for his money alone.

Medcalf was the owner of a series of book-binding companies and lived in Spitalfields where the book-binding industry was rife. He had inherited the business from his father and grandfather.

After a courtship of several months, he married Priscilla with her parents' blessing.

Despite the weight of his responsibilities, he was kind and chivalrous to his dainty bride and denied her nothing, so attracted was he to her modesty, her agreeable personality and her desire to raise a family without asking for any other favours.

Some would say that Priscilla was dull. Her engaging, white-toothed smile, her permanent consideration for Medcalf's needs and comforts and her dog-like devotion, devoid of showiness, endeared him to her even more. It was her beauty, combined with her very reticence which filled him with a love of which he had thought himself incapable.

One February morning, when all the lakes and ponds on the outskirts of London were frozen, he came down to breakfast euphoric and beaming. He kissed Priscilla on the cheek. He said. 'Did you know I've got two pairs of skates, left to me by my father who had the same shoe size as me?'

Priscilla looked up from her poetry book.

'I had no idea you liked skating.'

'Yes, this is a perfect morning for it. I could teach you if you like. I could fill the second pair of skates with cotton wool to suit your size. There are a few ponds just outside London. We could take the carriage there. Do tell me you'd like to come.'

'But I've got no sense of balance, Rupert.'

'It doesn't matter. I could hold your hand. You've never tried it. You'd love it.'

Priscilla lowered her head into her book once more.

'I'm sorry, Rupert. The idea doesn't appeal to me. No one knows how thick the ice is. Once you fall through it, you drown in the icy cold water underneath it. If you want to go, go alone.'

Medcalf brought his skates downstairs and gave orders for his coachman, Mr Freshwater, to wait for him outside.

'Take me to that pond we were talking about the other day, just outside London, Freshwater.'

'That I will, sir.'

Freshwater took his employer to a pond in Chelsea, then in the country. A watery sun shone through the sky, causing the pond to shine like a mirror. Because it was only 9.00 a.m. very few skaters were on the pond.

Medcalf got out of the carriage and advanced towards the pond. He removed his shoes and put on his skates before stepping onto the ice. The experience delighted him. He crossed the pond, weaving in figures of eight, singing with joy.

So euphoric was his mood, as he looked at the leafless trees surrounding the pond, that he failed to notice the ice breaking beneath him. It was only when the freezing water enveloped him that he realised his well-being was shortlived. As he sank into the water and felt every nerve in his body go numb, he thrust his arm like a ramrod through the ice, into the air, calling Priscilla's name.

* * *

Priscilla had been sitting by Jack's side while being haunted by the memory of Medcalf's death. The news was broken to her by Freshwater, whose lower-than-normal voice and bowed head indicated that serious harm had come to her husband.

Jack placed his hand on hers.

'How did your husband die, Priscilla?'

She told him what had happened. He noticed her cheeks were wet with tears. He licked the tears from her face, enchanted by the sight of a vulnerable woman weeping.

There was a pause and then he said, 'I'm enjoying your company. Priscilla. I'd like to meet you again here tomorrow. The best time would be half past four.'

'All right, Jack, tomorrow.'

When they had eaten, Jack escorted Priscilla to her carriage in the drive. He helped her in and kissed her hand before Freshwater cracked his whip, driving the four horses into the night.

Ethelred came out of the inn and rushed towards his brother.

'Will she be your new lady love?' he asked.

Jack detected jealousy in his voice.

'I hope so, Ethelred. Her name's Priscilla. I may have to leave you to play alone in the taverns tomorrow night. I hope I'll be able to spend the whole evening with her.'

'Where will that leave me?'

Jack's mood changed abruptly from one of contentment and amiability to one of surliness.

'See sense, Ethelred. You know very well you had a woman once and you left me alone to help Mother clean the cottage. If I want to woo a woman, I'll do so. Besides, no woman will ever come between us. We have and always will put our devotion to each other before our love for any woman, however charming and attractive she is.'

The brothers slapped each other on the back simultaneously but their action was not long enough to be an embrace.

'I'm meeting her here tomorrow at half past four, Ethelred,' Jack said.

The brothers walked slowly back to their lodgings on the wharf.

*   *   *

The following afternoon, Priscilla looked radiant. She was wearing a pale blue silk dress. Her hair was coiffed in ringlets and decorated with pale blue velvet ribbon. There was little conversation during dinner. She and Jack sat looking at each other.

Tea was brought to the table at the end of dinner. Their hands were shaking so much that they could hardly lift their cups to their lips. Jack was the first to speak.

'Where do you live, Priscilla?'

'Three miles away in Brominster Street.'

Brominster Street was affluent, unlike the rest of Spitalfields. The grand houses there had sometimes been burgled by the McArandys' friends from the wharf, a fact discomforting to Jack who hoped that Priscilla's was not among them.

'I hope you lock everything up and that you have bars on your windows. I'm told there are a lot of burglaries in that street because of the fine properties and the leafy trees which help cover the thieves when they get away.'

'How do you know this?'

'Word gets round. This is not too big a neighbourhood.'

As they left the inn, just before Priscilla was due to get into her carriage, she turned to Jack, her face wet with tears and plucked him by the sleeve.

'May I ask you something, Jack?'

'Why, yes. Ask me whatever you like.'

64

'I'm afraid to go home alone. Will you come with me?'

'With pleasure. Is there no one in the house to look after you?'

'Yes. A cook and my maid. They go to bed early. I am being very forward, I know, more so than becomes my sex, but I would like you to come.'

Jack helped Priscilla into the carriage and got in beside her. He ran his hands through her hair and kissed her. Although this was what she wanted, her brazenness made her feel shy.

She and Jack entered the house and walked up to her bedroom which was predominantly yellow. Yellow silk drapes surrounded the large four-poster bed in the centre of the room, which somehow made the room look colder.

Jack took her hands in his and said, 'You're very cold, aren't you? That is what I am here for, to make you warm. I don't want you to be shy.'

Rupert Medcalf's style between the sheets had always been soft and gentle. Although his foreplay had been sophisticated and rousing, his performance of the act itself had disappointed Priscilla by its unusual brevity. This had never cast a blight on the happiness of their marriage, because Priscilla had not attached much importance to the physical relationship, except when she had wanted to conceive. It had been Medcalf's personality, rather than his sexuality which had entranced her.

There had been times when she had regretted the extreme gentleness of his coital technique. Because she had always been a woman of low self-esteem, a subconscious masochism within her had sometimes caused her to yearn for a wilder, rougher and more forceful lover who could stay longer within her and maul her savagely throughout his stay.

It was Jack McArandy who came into this category as if Providence had sent him to her. He carried her to her bed, where he kissed her violently on the mouth, inserting his tongue, urgently untying the ribbons in her hair and removing her clothes. This, he did with the combination of the deft delicacy of an experienced lover and evident frustration when he had to undo the intricate laces in the corset she had on.

Once he had removed her clothes, he only removed the parts of his own clothes to make an act of sex possible. If ambiguously, he felt it insulting to appear naked in front of a woman on their first night together.

He ran his hands violently all over her, breathing heavily with a slight wheeze. His initial entry was reasonably gentle. As she screamed in ecstasy, he pumped himself in and out of her like an untamed horse out of control. Although it took him 15 minutes to finish, she was in a permanent state of ejaculation and shouted and screamed frenziedly as if in pain.

They rolled onto their sides, exhausted. Jack was the first to speak.

'Do you always come like that?' he asked.

'Never before. It was wonderful when you put your weight on your arms. Rupert never did that.'

'I'm not interested in Rupert or in what he did,' he said abruptly, adding, 'I adore you, Priscilla, you're like a little doll. I want to go on doing this to you for ever.'

* * *

The following day, regardless of the disgust of the servants who, fortunately, had no idea who the McArandys were, Jack moved into the house with his new love whose candour, radiance and reticence reminded him of his mother. In the evenings, he continued to play with Ethelred at the taverns, finishing at The Fife and Drum.

'When will you take me to the taverns?' Priscilla asked one morning at breakfast.

'They're no place for a lady,' he said, 'but late tomorrow night I will have a surprise for you.'

The next night he brought his violin home and sang *Greensleeves* for her. His silvery voice, the like of which she had never heard before, stirred her and deepened her adoration for him.

They got into bed and Priscilla asked, 'Have you ever had it in mind to marry me?'

'No. That can never be. You are rich and I am poor. It would not be fair on you or your husband's memory. For a man to marry he must be financially superior to his wife. Otherwise he would be dishonouring her.'

'I don't mind being dishonoured.'

Jack ran his hands through her hair.

'I do mind,' he said, 'but I still want to live with you.'

Priscilla was relieved at least to hear that, but his refusal to marry her, combined with the disapproving looks of her servants, humiliated and vexed her. She secretly made up her mind to conceive.

They lived in this way for several months and had violent, uninhibited sex two or three times a day. Still, she had not conceived but she became less obsessive about her wish.

Within ten months she began to feel ill and was sick each morning. Jack sent for a physician and stood outside the room while he examined her.

'What's wrong with her?' he asked.

He remembered his mother's illness and the fear of losing Priscilla made him sick with worry.

'It can be one of two things,' the physician said.

'Whatever do you mean?'

'A boy or a girl.'

'You mean I'm to be a father?'

'Yes, sir. You're to be a father,' replied the physician.

* * *

67

When the brothers met at The Fife and Drum Ethelred looked lonely and dejected, particularly as Jack was looking so overjoyed.

'I'm going to be a father, Ethelred.'

Ethelred pretended to be pleased.

'Congratulations. Are you going to marry Priscilla?'

'How can I possibly, given who I am and who she is? It wouldn't be fair to a kindly gentlewoman like her. She's not some whore like the woman you used to visit. She's good and decent, like Mother.'

'Isn't that all the more reason to marry her, when you're going to be the father of her child?'

'It wouldn't be right or fair, either to her or the child. What if I were to be hauled in?'

'But you wouldn't need to rob any more. You'd get her money,' said Ethelred.

'I may have broken the law in my life. I may have stolen and killed, but nothing in the world would induce me to take money from a woman I respect.'

Priscilla was waiting for Jack when he came home.

'You've had the dressmaker here, haven't you?' he said smiling.

'How do you know?'

'I saw the dress in the dressing room, ready for you to try on. It's finished, isn't it?'

'You're more observant than I thought.'

'I love red silk. How did you know red was my favourite colour?'

'I know everything about you.'

'No, you don't. If you did, you wouldn't want to marry me.'

'Is the thing I don't know the thing that is stopping you?'

'Yes.'

'Then you owe it to me to tell me.'

Jack raised his voice in anger. It was the first time she had heard him do this and it startled her.

'I don't have to tell you all my business, Priscilla. You have no right to make such demands on me. You also have no right to expect me to marry you just because you're with child. If you go on harassing me, I will refuse to go on living here.'

'No gentleman refuses to marry the mother of his child,' she said quietly.

'I am no gentleman!' he shouted.

'No, Jack, I don't think you are.'

He slapped her face but took care not to do this too violently. She fell to the floor. He picked her up and laid her on the bed.

'I'm sleeping on the couch tonight, Priscilla. I'm not blaming you but I have a lot on my mind.'

She rolled over onto her stomach and wept.

* * *

Ethelred was walking home to the wharf when he was accosted by a ragged, hysterical, emaciated woman, shouting and talking gibberish. Her face was sunken like a skull's and her clothes, or what remained of them, were falling off her body. He saw that she was starving and hardly able to stand. He held her to prevent her from falling. All he could understand from her garbled speech were the words 'Help me,' which she repeated several times.

'Sally!' he exclaimed.

'Yes. That's right. Help me, Ethelred. I've been robbed of the few pennies I had. I've had nothing to eat for three days.'

'You'd better come with me. I'll give you something to eat and you'll be able to lie down for the night.'

Sally clung to his arm.

'Oh, Ethelred, you're a gentleman in every sense of the word.'

'No, Sally. Not a gentleman. Just a man.'

Tom, the burglar, and Freddie took pity on the starving waif Ethelred had brought back. Both gave her the sausages which they would otherwise have eaten themselves. They were horrified by the way she wolfed them down without chewing them.

Ethelred turned to Tom.

'Can Sally stay here until we fatten her up a bit? After that, I can take her back to the room I'm still paying rent for, where we used to live.'

'You know she can stay here as long as she needs to,' said Tom.

Ethelred's pity of Sally was transformed to the love he bore her in the past, and he tolerated it when she bedded both Tom and Freddie to earn a few pennies. He regarded it as her way of contributing towards the rent and even felt ennobled by her actions at first.

* * *

Within two weeks she put on weight, although she remained thin. With her earnings she was able to buy some cheap dresses and shawls in the Spitalfields market.

Ethelred waited for Tom, Freddie and the others to leave the building before speaking to her.

'You can't go on living here, Sally. I know you're trying to help with the rent but I don't want you to go on bedding Tom and Freddie when I'm in the same room. Besides, it's not very comfortable here. I've still got our little room. Wouldn't you prefer to come back to your old home?'

'Oh, Ethelred, you're so forgiving!'

'No, I'm not. I'm very lonely at the moment and could do with a woman's company. I know I lost my temper with you that day but I'm prepared to forget what happened. I'll give you some money every week to buy food and anything else we both need as I'm earning more now. All I ask is that you cook my supper after I come home late in the evenings. Anything would be better than your way of life. Will you come?'

'All right, Ethelred. I'll come. You are a gentleman at heart. I know that.'

* * *

Priscilla sobbed herself to sleep the night she had quarrelled with Jack. She felt jaded and depleted when she woke up in her dress supported by an agonisingly tight corset. Jack did not know how to handle hysterically crying women as it embarrassed and depressed him. He woke up before Priscilla who found him kneeling by the bed.

He took her hand in his and said, 'I was dreadful to you last night. I should never have behaved like that towards a decent and beautiful gentlewoman whom I respect and love. I treated you like a street harlot and have nothing to say to defend myself. I'd understand it if you wanted me to leave. Do you have it in you to forgive me, or would you like me to go away?'

She noticed that his almond-shaped dark eyes were moist.

She realised she was even more in love with him than before and said, 'Of course I forgive you, Jack. We all lose our tempers sometimes and I was nagging you beyond endurance. I couldn't live without you and although I accept that you cannot marry me, for whatever reason, I would like you to be with me when the baby is born. I know you can never be my husband, but you would be a wonderful father and if it is not too much to ask you, I would like it if you could help me raise our baby. Will you be there for me, Jack?'

Jack didn't answer immediately and got into bed without removing his clothes.

'I'll be there, Priscilla. I'll be there for as long as you want me to be. I want the baby as much as you do and I want to be with you, watching it grow up. What do you hope for, a son or a daughter?'

71

Priscilla had been lying on top of the bed until then. She got under the covers without removing her clothes because Jack had not removed his.

'I want a son,' she said, 'not a daughter.'

'How assertive you sound! Why don't you want a daughter?'

She leant over and embraced him.

'Because I want another Jack McArandy,' she said.

His love for her was such that he had tears in his eyes.

He said, 'How do you feel about turning top to bottom?'

She raised herself, putting her weight on her elbows.

'What does that mean?' she asked.

'Oh, dear. It's most indelicate to explain. I don't want to be rough with you when you're with child, so I suggest you put your head on the pillow, and I put my head at the bottom of the bed.'

'Oh, I understand. We lick each other.'

'That is correct, my little doll. Let's undress.'

Priscilla was overwhelmed with happiness the next day. She delighted Jack by wearing her red dress. Until he had to go the taverns that evening, she taught him to play backgammon. Later on he sat and watched her radiantly as she worked on her tapestry, which showed multi-coloured spring flowers, before studying his music sheets. He never sight-read music. Instead, he examined the score and learnt it by heart if it was too difficult to play by ear.

That evening, Jack had been away from the house for an hour and a half and Priscilla lay on the bed, still wearing her red silk dress to please him on his return.

She was reading a leather-bound edition of works by the metaphysical poets, whose vulnerable, if effete, romanticism stirred her and reminded her of Jack's love for her and hers for him.

Her pleasure was interrupted by a knock on the door. It was Mathilda, her maid who had served her throughout her marriage to her first husband and whom she liked and trusted.

It was unusual for Mathilda to come to her room without being summoned by the bell.

'Is something amiss, Mathilda?'

' 'Tis a grave matter, ma'am,' replied Mathilda. 'I know 'tis unusual to come to your bedroom without being asked, but I feel I must ask your permission to sit down.'

'Why, yes. Are you in trouble?'

'Oh, ma'am, 'tis a matter of some grievous weight.'

'All right. Sit down. I slept badly last night so I am rather tired. Would you please keep it brief.'

Mathilda was frightened, although she was not usually in awe of the gentle Priscilla. She staggered to an upright seventeenth-century chair and sat down, leaning forward as if in pain.

' 'Tis my duty to warn you that you are in great danger, ma'am,' she said.

'Of what?' said Priscilla impatiently.

Her pregnancy was making her feel nauseated, tired and dizzy.

Mathilda fidgeted in the uncomfortable chair.

'When I'm off duty, ma'am, I go for walks through this neighbourhood. I know a lot of people in these parts and I know the area very well. I hear things that are said and what troubles me is that I hear the same things from many different people, none of them related.'

Priscilla yawned. She wished Mathilda would leave the room so that she could continue reading and was not interested in her maid's words. She thought she was about to talk about necromancy and witchcraft.

'All right, Mathilda, tell me what you heard.'

Mathilda wrung her hands and continued to fidget.

'I have only your interests at heart, ma'am, having served you for so long. I'm afraid it concerns Mr McArandy.'

'Mr McArandy?' exclaimed Priscilla, sitting bolt upright on the bed.

'Yes, ma'am. He's not the good man he seems to you. He has committed evil acts. He has done more than one murder and bludgeoned and tortured his victims. The only reason he and his brother have not been hauled in is that everyone is terrified of them, and also they give so much pleasure as musicians.'

'This is outrageous!' exclaimed Priscilla. 'I'm having his child.'

'Oh, ma'am! And he hasn't even asked you to marry him. You must get rid of it somehow. To bring another McArandy into the world would be unthinkable, dangerous and downright wicked. The many people I've spoken to say there's insanity in the McArandy family, going back for generations. You love this man because you are blind. I know how long I have served you, but I will have no choice but to leave your employ if further evil is brought to this house.'

Priscilla got off the bed and walked over to Mathilda. Despite her gentleness, she looked towering and formidable in her full-length red dress. She raised her voice in anger.

'I have had as much as I can take from you, Mathilda. How dare you speak to me like that about Mr McArandy who is to be the father of my child! You make vague references to people you have spoken to in this neighbourhood but you are unable to give the names of any of these people. Kindly provide me with their names.'

'I don't know their names, ma'am.'

'Where did you meet them, in the street?'

'Yes, ma'am. Clusters of people gather together and start talking.'

'You have no idea who these people are, do you?'

74

'No, ma'am. They don't have to give their names to tell the truth.'

'What makes you think their remarks are no more than prejudiced rumours, circulated through jealousy because Jack and Ethelred are so talented that they always have money in their pockets and because, despite their humble background, they speak educated English?'

Mathilda continued to wring her hands.

'But ma'am, it's all true. Someone saw them both throwing the body of a man they had murdered into the Thames. The body of a man with red hair and a red beard.'

'Someone? Someone? You're going to have to do better than that. Who, Mathilda?'

'Oh, just someone passing by. In fact, it was someone who saw someone else.'

Priscilla was tempted to hit Mathilda. She held her hands behind her back to prevent herself from doing so.

'Mathilda, I am very tired, partly because I slept badly last night and partly because I am with child. I've heard what you have to say and in no circumstances do I wish to hear any more. Had you not been in my employ for so many years. I would not have hesitated to dismiss you with an unfavourable reference. I want you to leave this room immediately.'

Mathilda had difficulty rising from the upright wooden chair because she had been sitting there for so long that her back was stiff. She walked towards the door as if to leave the room and suddenly turned to face her employer.

'I'll leave the room, ma'am, and as soon as I find a new situation I am leaving your employ. I do not care to remain in this household while a man like Mr McArandy is living here.'

Priscilla was relieved to be deprived of the company of a woman who had spoken to her in such a disturbing manner. She tried desperately to ignore information which was not accompanied by facts, but she knew how much Mathilda cared for her, which was her reason for daring to approach her to talk about Jack. She asked herself why these rumours could have been circulated if Jack was really as exemplary as he appeared. She remembered his words, 'If you knew everything about me you would not wish to marry me,' and shuddered.

She went downstairs to the drawing-room and poured herself half a glass of brandy, which she drained in one go before realising she had had too much. She went back to her bedroom and lay down, feeling dizzier than before.

Gradually the dizziness lessened and her mood became elevated. She told herself she was a fool to be taken in by street gossip, together with the vagueness of Mathilda's words. Her doubts dispelled and her adulation of Jack flooded through her mind once more. She was glad to be wearing a dress which was his favourite colour and a feeling of peace and security descended on her.

Then her thoughts turned to her faithful Mathilda and the idea of her leaving filled her with horror. Until now she had taken Mathilda for granted, assuming she would work for her indefinitely.

Because of her lighthearted mood, she decided she would talk to Mathilda the following day and was convinced she would persuade her to change her mind. She planned to speak to her kindly and if this failed she told herself she would refuse to give Mathilda a reference, thus preventing her from finding another situation.

Now that her mind was relaxed, she re-opened her book of the works of the metaphysical poets but they failed to stimulate her as much as before. She thought of the effete poets who had penned the verses she read, and compared them with Jack's robust build, masculinity and uninhibited roughness as a lover. She was seized by a further surge adoration for Jack. She drifted into a peaceful sleep until she was woken on his return, when he was as loving as always and delicately placed round her neck a gold necklace which he had stolen.

He patted her on the stomach and remarked, 'You're beginning to swell up a bit, aren't you my girl?'

'Yes, but I sometimes feel so sick and dizzy.'

'Do you want to go to sleep?'

'No. I'm wide awake. I'd rather go down to the drawing-room and have a drink.'

'I can refuse you nothing, particularly in your own house. Would you like a game of backgammon?'

As Priscilla had a love for that game she was pleased that Jack had suggested it. It was almost as if he were able to read her mind.

They played three games. Each time, Jack let her win because he knew she was unwell and wished to humour her. They went to bed at 2.00 a.m. They stripped naked and slept in each other's arms and kissed each other violently, putting their tongues in each other's mouths.

Just before they went to sleep, Jack said, 'Will you wear that lovely dress again tomorrow, Priscilla?'

'Of course I will and the necklace too.'

* * *

Priscilla felt unwell and slept for most of the following day. Jack sat by her bedside in case she needed him. By the time he had left for the taverns she was wide awake.

Again she was alerted by a knock on the door. It was Mathilda. She bit her lip to prevent herself from losing her temper with her.

'Come in, Mathilda. Sit down in your usual chair.'

'I don't need to sit down, ma'am.'

'Well, what is it?'

'I've come to apologise for my shocking behaviour last night and about them things I said about Mr McArandy. He came to the pantry for some cake today and he talked to me so kindly. A proper gentleman he is, ma'am. I should never have listened to rumours. Them street gossips can be so cruel, can't they, ma'am?'

Priscilla smiled. She went over to Mathilda and put her arm round her.

'Don't worry. I've already forgiven you. Will you stay?'

'Yes, ma'am, I'll stay.'

Priscilla and Jack were very happy for the next few weeks. As the nausea and dizziness wore off she became increasingly excited about the birth of her child. They spent their mornings playing backgammon, which she nearly always won, and Jack taught her some card games. She had no flair for card games and even when he tried to let her win she lost.

In the afternoons she went to bed and Jack lay down with her to keep her company. He noticed that although she was always happy and smiling, she seemed fragile and pale and in permanent need of rest. This reminded him of his mother and caused him to be even more protective and paternal towards her than before.

One day after her rest he told her he was worried about her frailty, which seemed unnatural to him because she was eating plenty of nutritious food.

He said, 'How would you like me to take you out in the carriage and then have a walk near the Thames? We could take a loaf of bread and feed the gulls and terns. It would bring some colour into your cheeks. I think you are tired and pale because you never go outdoors and you never get any fresh air.'

Jack had become overtly reckless because he had never been caught red-handed committing crimes. It did not occur to him that Richard Hetherington, the Hertfordshire country squire, who knew of his identity from Edward Hulton, the coachman, was still pursuing him, backed by the local landowners. He also had no idea that he and Ethelred had been seen by a neighbour dragging George Robertson away from Tinley Street.

As for the theft of the ring from the shop, when a passerby in the street had recognised the two well-known musicians, this was something Jack was unaware of. Besides, it flattered his vanity to be seen arm-in-arm with a smart pregnant women, walking near the banks of the Thames.

Jack and Priscilla laughed as they broke up pieces of bread and fed them to the birds. They were amused by the way they formed in clusters as they competed for the last piece.

'It reminds me of life, Priscilla,' Jack said. 'There's so little of what is good that some of us fight for our lives just to get a little of it.'

'Have you had to do that, Jack?'

'Of course I have. I was born poor and I've had to fight all my life to survive.'

'It makes me feel so guilty that you have known hardship. I've had everything I could possibly want all my life. I have never had any idea what it's like to be poor. Sometimes, I wish I did.'

Jack kissed her on the cheek.

'Don't blame yourself, Priscilla. It's not your fault you're rich. Anyway, I can't complain now. I've got you.'

The following afternoon, when they went to feed the birds, the river was calm and a pleasantly warm, pale sun emerged from behind a cloud. Jack knew there was something Priscilla wanted by the wistful look in her eyes.

He held her hand and turned to her.

'What can I do for you, my little doll?'

'I'd like to go on the river on a boat. It bores me to have to go in the carriage every day. What I'd really like is for you to somehow get hold of a boat. What I'd like most of all is to end up in one of those coffee shops in Fleet Street, where the writers and intellectuals go.'

Jack laughed.

'What's so funny?' she asked.

'My dear girl, very few pleasure boats travel on the Thames these days because of its severely neglected banks. Besides, there would be a dreadful smell if we went much closer to the river than we are now. But here's some good news. We'll take the carriage to a Fleet Street coffee shop, where we'll see all sorts of writers and poets coming in and out.'

'Oh, I should love that.'

'Before we go, I'll tell you about the river. Mother always told Ethelred and me about that icy winter when it froze over. It was the scene of a busy fair with swing-boats and dancing bears. Let's hope next winter is like that.'

'I'd like that. We could try one of the swing-boats,' said Priscilla.

They went to feed the birds every afternoon after Priscilla's rest and gradually some colour came to her cheeks.

One afternoon, as they were feeding the birds, they noticed an old man doing the same thing, standing 20 feet away. Priscilla was the first to notice his presence and there was something about him which chilled and frightened her.

He wore brown breeches and a brown waistcoat with a white shirt underneath and his clothes were filthy, torn and ragged. He had long, thinning grey hair which was untidy and scraped back from his face in a pony-tail. The most sinister aspect of his appearance was his abnormally piercing, pale blue eyes with their prominent black pupils which were fixed menacingly on Priscilla.

'What's the matter, Priscilla?' asked Jack. 'If you don't feel well, we'll go home.'

'It's that man,' said Priscilla. 'He keeps staring at me in a horrible sort of way.'

'What man?' asked Jack, who had not noticed the newcomer until then.

'The man on our right. The one with the grey hair.'

80

Jack looked to the right, at the man who averted his gaze.

'What's wrong with him? He's just an old man feeding the birds.'

'He's not just feeding the birds. He keeps looking at me.'

Jack studied the man at periodic intervals. Suddenly he noticed he was indeed staring at Priscilla and that his eyes, with their piercing pupils, were so pale they could have belonged to an albino.

'Wait here, will you,' said Jack.

'No. Please don't leave me alone.'

'I'll have to. I'm going over to have a word with him.'

Jack went up to the old man and stood a foot away from him.

'What do you mean by staring at my wife?'

The old man said nothing and stared at Jack, without speaking.

'Will you kindly stop staring at her. She is nervous and unwell,' said Jack, before turning away to walk back to Priscilla.

'Oh, Jack, I feel so unwell. Will you take me home?'

'Yes, of course I'll take you home.'

He put both his hands onto her shoulders, and kissed her.

Just as they approached the house, Priscilla turned round and saw the old man standing behind her. Her fear turned to rage.

'Who are you and what do you want of me? First you stare at me. Then you follow me to my house.'

Jack was impressed by her feistiness and decided not to say anything. He wanted Priscilla to think she was able to look after herself without being permanently dependent on him.

The man advanced towards her with his palms outstretched. She noticed they were completely black and had a strange, musty smell which alarmed her.

'All I want is a wee loaf of bread,' he said, failing to avert his eyes from hers.

He spoke with a strange accent she had never heard before. It was harsh, nasal and clipped. It was a Scottish accent.

'Is that really all you want? Is that why you've been staring at me?'

'It's bread I want for now,' he said.

'Wait outside. I'll get you a loaf of bread.'

Jack considered the man harmless and went upstairs. Priscilla went into the house and fetched a loaf of bread from the kitchen before going out into the street. She handed it to the man and turned abruptly to go back into the house.

The man let out a hollow laugh as he tapped her on the shoulder.

'Yes, what is it?'

'I know where you live now,' he said. He continued to fix her with his terrifying stare. ' 'Tis not the first time I'll be coming to your house. I'll be back sometime when you're least expecting me, when you're alone and it will be something else I'll be wanting then.'

'You certainly won't be coming to my house ever again. Not only that, I am never alone here. I shall simply give a description of you to the people in the house and I shall issue instructions that you are not to come in!' she shouted because she wanted Jack to hear her, knowing he would be impressed by her show of spirit.

She went through the front door and tried to close it but the man put his foot in the way.

'Remove your foot this instant or I shall call for Jack.'

'So Jack *is* the name of the man who was with you feeding the birds?'

'Yes. Jack McArandy, to be precise. McArandy, the celebrated musician.'

'Now, I know. He'll swing one day all right. He'll swing.'

The doubts which had once flooded through her mind returned. She remembered Mathilda's words about Jack and shuddered. She forced herself to ignore them and kicked the man in the shin. He removed his foot but held the door open with his hand. She threw her weight against the door and slammed it, hurting his fingers.

She went upstairs to the bedroom where Jack was lying on the couch, laughing.

'I've never heard such spirit in my life, my girl,' he said, 'and what impresses me most is the fact that you're feeling unwell. Am I right in thinking that you gave that man my name?'

'Yes, I told him who you are.'

'I wish you hadn't done that.'

'Why?'

'Because a lot of people round here don't care for me and I don't want anyone to know I'm living here.'

'Why don't they care for you?'

'I think you'll remember we had a similar conversation before which ended in tears. I'm not the man you see me as. I've done a lot of wrong in my life in order to survive and also to help Mother to raise money when she needed a surgeon.'

'What wrong have you done, Jack? It won't make any difference to me.'

'It's best you don't know, for your own safety, but there's a risk I could get hauled in, so don't give any suspicious characters my name, or tell them where I live. Remember that whatever I've done, I'll still be the same person to you.'

Priscilla looked at him apprehensively but tried to hide her expression.

'All right, Jack. I really don't want to know what you did, but that man who wanted bread from the house told me you'd swing one day.'

Jack looked more amused than shocked.

'Perhaps I will, Priscilla, perhaps I will.'

'So it's as bad as that, is it?'

Jack got irritated.

'You just told me you didn't want to hear about the things I had done. Now you ask me questions. If you don't want to know, and I don't want you to know, kindly don't ask.'

She hated it when Jack was angry. She took his hand in hers.

'All right, Jack. I won't ask again. It's none of my business. As long as you're good to me, I couldn't care less what you did in the past.'

Jack ran his hands through her hair and kissed her.

'Let's go down and have a game of backgammon,' he said.

* * *

When Jack went out that evening, Priscilla lay on the bed, obsessively wondering what he had done. She remembered Mathilda's words, 'He has done more than one murder and bludgeoned and tortured his victims,' and the strange old man's words, 'He'll swing one day.'

She told herself that a kindly, chivalrous man like Jack could not possibly have murdered anyone. When he had told her he had done wrong to survive and to raise money to find a surgeon for his sick mother, she had assumed that he had merely stolen.

While thinking about it afterwards she concluded that she was unfairly privileged and throughout her life had wanted for nothing. She felt guilty because of her lover's poverty in contrast with her affluence and understood why a poor person should have to steal to survive and pay a surgeon to treat his mother.

She wondered whether he had ever used violence in desperation for money and told herself that perhaps in certain circumstances the use of violence was essential for survival.

Over all, she felt ennobled by her thoughts but cursed herself for not having the courage to fight for survival, had she been born poor. She felt worthless and inadequate and despised herself. As her love for Jack continued to solidify, and her doubts about him diminished, so her hatred for herself increased, as well as her shame of her riches.

She even wondered whether she should give all her money away, if only to test her endurance and give herself self-confidence, by having to struggle and prove to herself that she could survive.

She thought of mothers with no money giving birth and letting their babies fall to the floor as a matter of course, while bending over a bowl, doing a day's washing.

She knew she would not have to be delivered of her infant in that manner. Mathilda, who had been a midwife years ago before she worked for her, would assist with the birth. Priscilla would not be bending over doing a day's washing while the infant fell to the floor.

As these thoughts went through her head, she became sadder and sadder and began to cry until Jack returned.

'What is it, my girl?'

'Oh, Jack, I'm so ashamed.'

'Ashamed? Of what?'

'Of the fact that you are poor and I am rich and have never had to struggle to survive.'

'But you're a gentlewoman. No one can expect you to struggle. You're fragile and delicate. You're too good to lead a rough, brutal life.'

'I feel so guilty, not having to work when you have to struggle.'

Jack went downstairs and brought her some Cognac which he pressed to her lips.

'What you must understand is that I was born in poverty and never had riches, although I have enough to live on now. If you'd been born in poverty you would not have known any other life. You would have fought your situation, and there is more fight in you than you know, but you wouldn't have had time to brood the way you do. You brood too much and you spend too much time lying down thinking about yourself. You should get up and about more.'

'But I get melancholy sometimes because of the baby and I get exhausted,' she said.

'You told me that since the early stage was over you've been feeling a lot better.'

'Occasionally, I feel better but how can my spirits be raised if I have nothing to do?'

'During the day you have more than enough to do. We play games together, including backgammon which you seem to enjoy. You appear to like our afternoon walks. You also love what we both like doing best. I know you're alone in the evenings when I'm working, but you still have plenty to do besides lie down, just thinking.'

'But what can I do when you're working? Your hours are so long.'

'No, they are not. They are half-past six to half-past ten. Four hours only. Then of course I have to talk to Ethelred, whom I don't see much of, and have a few tankards of ale. I'm always back by half-past eleven.'

'That makes five hours,' said Priscilla. 'How can I occupy my time for five hours?'

Jack was becoming impatient, but he knew Priscilla was frail and heavily weighed down with her infant eight months after conception.

He said, 'Firstly, there's your tapestry that you could work on. I notice you've neglected this of late. You've only filled in three of the spring flowers and you've got a lot more work to do before you finish it.

'Then you've got your poetry books to read. You told me the other day that you had a favourite book of poets referred to by some funny name.'

'You mean the metaphysical poets?'

'That's right. Have you got bored with them?'

'Yes. The characters I see in those poems are not as muscular and masculine as you. They disappoint me.'

'God bless you, my girl!' Jack said, obviously touched, adding, 'You've got other books to read, haven't you, all in fine leather bindings?'

'I've read them all, Jack.'

'I'm beginning to get very bored with all this, Priscilla,' said Jack. 'One thing I can't stand is a woman who is always whining and complaining that she hasn't enough to do. I don't understand why you don't get on with your needlework. I shall expect to see your tapestry finished by the end of the week. Otherwise I shall be very disappointed. You wouldn't want to disappoint me, would you?'

'No, Jack.'

'So do you promise to finish it by the end of the week? Today is Friday. I want it finished by the following Friday.'

'All right, Jack. I'll do it, just for you. There's one thing I have wanted to ask you for a long time.'

'Which is what?'

'I would so much like to meet your brother, Ethelred.'

'Would you? Why?'

'Because he's your brother. He's dear to you, I know, and he's a part of you.'

'Why didn't you ask me before?'

'Because I was too shy.'

'It's your shyness that attracts me. I don't see why you shouldn't meet Ethelred. I'll ask him to come over one morning. Would you like that?'

Priscilla embraced him.

'Oh, yes! You're so good to me, Jack.'

*   *   *

It was on Sunday morning that Ethelred visited the house, having been given directions by Jack.

Priscilla and Jack were waiting for him in the drawing room. She was wearing a pink satin dress which accentuated her blonde hair.

'Priscilla, this is Ethelred,' said Jack.

Ethelred bent over and kissed her hand.

'How do you do, my lady?'

'No. Not "my lady". Call me Priscilla,' she said shyly.

Unlike Jack, Ethelred was as shy as Priscilla. At that moment, Jack was unsure which one he loved most.

'Sorry, I should have said "Priscilla",' said Ethelred.

He took two steps backwards and stood stiffly like a soldier. Then he formed his right hand into a fist, raised it to his mouth and gave a discreet little cough.

'Don't stand there like that, Ethelred, sit down,' said Jack.

Ethelred was about to sit down next to Priscilla but sat on an adjacent chair instead.

'I know it's only 11.00 o'clock in the morning, but I think we should all have a drink,' said Jack.

'What will you have?' asked Priscilla.

'Some gin, please if you have it,' said Ethelred.

Gin was not a favourite drink of Priscilla's but Jack liked it and often drank it before going to sleep.

'Priscilla, give Ethelred some gin,' said Jack, 'and I'll have some as well. What are you going to have?'

'Red wine.'

The three drank in silence. Ethelred was worried because he thought he wasn't grand enough for Priscilla. Jack was worried because he feared Priscilla might find Ethelred awkward and slow-witted. Priscilla was worried because she feared Ethelred's shyness and thought he would be unable to speak to her after she had been looking forward to meeting him.

They all drank quickly and filled their glasses, still without speaking. They repeated this procedure until they had each had four glasses and the tension in the room disappeared.

'How about a game of cards?' suggested Jack.

They settled down at the card table and played a card game whose rules were easy and straightforward. Ethelred was able to laugh and joke when he knew he was winning. Priscilla and Jack felt relaxed and happy.

Priscilla said, 'I can hardly tell the difference between the two of you.'

'You haven't noticed my blond streak, have you?' said Ethelred, adding, 'I feel in the mood for a game of blind man's bluff.'

'Don't be an idiot, Ethelred,' said Jack. 'Priscilla is with child and if she falls over she might lose it. You don't think, do you?'

Ethelred couldn't bear to be ticked off by Jack in front of any woman, let alone a grand lady. He remained seated with his head lowered, inadvertently drawing attention to his blond streak.

Priscilla sensed his mood immediately and pampered him by putting a cushion behind his back and pouring him more gin. Jack suddenly became jealous.

'She never gives me that kind of attention,' he said.

Ethelred sensed the onset of an unpleasant atmosphere. He rose drunkenly to his feet, telling his brother and Priscilla that he had to leave.

'That really is very irritating of you, Ethelred,' said Jack. 'Priscilla was looking forward to meeting you and you suddenly get up to leave just as we are all settling down. Not only that, I think you've been rather rude to her by leaving abruptly like this.'

'I'm so sorry, Priscilla,' muttered Ethelred.

The effects of the gin were beginning to wear off and his surroundings were unfamiliar and hateful to him. He shuffled downstairs towards the front door. Jack ran after him.

'I'm furious with you, Ethelred,' he said. 'You are to write a note of apology to Priscilla.'

'I did say I was sorry, Jack.'

'Saying sorry is not enough. You're to write her a note.'

'All right, I'll write her a note. I've never been to a big house like this and I've never met a grand lady before. You don't realise how shy I was feeling. I felt like an idiot.'

'You felt like an idiot because you are an idiot. You're not a child any more. You should learn to adapt to strange surroundings and if you can't adapt you should pretend to be at ease, even if you aren't. You have embarrassed me, Ethelred.'

Ethelred hated being a disappointment to his brother.

'I'm sorry, Jack,' he said.

Jack suddenly felt sorry for having admonished his brother and hugged him.

'Don't worry. It's all right, Ethelred.'

'We're still friends, aren't we?'

'We're much more than friends. We're brothers.'

Priscilla was still sitting when Jack entered the drawing room.

He said, 'I'm so sorry about Ethelred getting up to leave like that. He's not as worldly as me and he's very shy in the same way as you are. He's never been to a big house like this before and he just lost his nerve.'

She got up and poured herself another glass of wine. She had taken a liking to Ethelred and his sudden departure was a great disappointment to her.

She drained the glass of wine, her fifth that morning, and said, 'I didn't mind. I think he's so sweet and gentle.'

'Not as sweet and gentle as me, I hope,' Jack said urgently.

'No, Jack, not as sweet as you, but he does remind me of you and is a great comfort to me.'

'That's a charming thing to say.'

'I feel so relaxed now, I'd like another glass of wine.'

As she went to the cabinet to fill her glass, Jack took her by the arm and pulled her back, closing the cabinet.

'I can't let you have any more, my girl. The glass you wanted would have been your sixth. There's a danger it might damage the baby. That would break your heart as it would mine.'

The wine made Priscilla ill and she had to spend the afternoon in bed. Jack was irritated by her drinking and refused to stay in the room with her to comfort her. Instead, he went down to the drawing room and studied his music sheets.

He went up to see her when he had to go out and found she had nearly recovered from her drunkenness.

'I'm glad to see you are better, my girl, and I don't want to see you drinking again until the baby is born. Also, now that you are better, I want you to keep yourself occupied. When I come back tonight, I will inspect your needlework and I hope to see some progress.'

When Jack came back he inspected her needlework and noticed that she had filled in two more of the spring flowers, leaving four more to go.

'Good girl!' he said affectionately. 'This deserves a kiss. Take off all your clothes and I'll take off mine. We'll keep each other warm tonight.'

* * *

When Mathilda brought Priscilla and Jack their breakfast in bed the morning after Ethelred's visit, there was a hand-delivered letter on the tray addressed to Priscilla with neat, rather strained, copperplate writing on the envelope. She tore it open.

'That's Ethelred's writing, Priscilla,' said Jack. 'I'd be interested to hear what he has to say about his peculiar behaviour.'

Priscilla read it aloud.

Dear Priscilla,

I am writing to say that I am sorry about my bad manners towards you yesterday. Please understand, I did not mean to insult you. I have never met a real lady before. I am only a humble man and I felt unworthy of your company and your beautiful house.

I hope you will forgive my rudeness and boorishness in time.
I remain your obedient servant,
Ethelred McArandy.

'Isn't that a polite letter?' remarked Jack.

'Yes, it is, most touching. Your brother is such a kind man.'

'Indeed? Am I not kind?'

'Of course you are. You didn't need to ask that question. I wouldn't be having your child if you were not. Should I not write back to Ethelred?'

'There's no need. I have a telepathic relationship with him, even when we are apart. I often know exactly what he is thinking, whether he is happy, sad, angry or dejected. I also know he is aware of how much you appreciate his letter.'

*   *   *

Priscilla had been carrying her infant for just over eight months. Her spirits were higher, but the weight of the foetus exhausted her so she spent all her time in bed. She was optimistically convinced that she was going to bring another Jack McArandy into the world and no longer felt lonely when he went to the taverns in the evenings.

She had already finished her tapestry to please Jack and was lying on the bed one evening, working on a new one, showing a pastel-toned pastoral scene. She felt so contented within herself that she savoured the opportunity of being alone.

Her contentment was short-lived. Mathilda knocked on

the door and when she opened it she looked strange and agitated.

'Mathilda, I really do wish to be alone this evening,' her mistress said angrily.

Mathilda started wringing her hands, a habit which infuriated Priscilla.

'Ma'am,' she said hoarsely, ''tis a matter of very great urgency.'

Priscilla pointed to the upright, seventeenth-century chair, the most uncomfortable chair in the room. She preferred the verbose Mathilda to sit in this chair so that she would not wish to be seated for too long and would want to leave the room as soon as possible.

'I must insist on your being brief, Mathilda,' said Priscilla.

'Oh, ma'am, there's a very strange man in the house. When he banged on the door, I answered. I told him he could not come in, but he threw his weight against the door, knocking me to the floor.'

'Where is the man now?'

'I told him to leave but he stormed upstairs and found his way to the drawing-room. He wants to speak to you about a matter which he says is very important.'

Priscilla's immediate reaction was of fear that Jack had come to harm. She raised herself with a stupendous effort and rested her weight on her elbows.

'Has anything happened to Mr McArandy?' she asked hurriedly. 'Has he been hurt?'

'No, ma'am.'

'In that case, you will please tell him that I have gone to bed because I am indisposed. Kindly ask him to leave immediately.'

She paused for a moment, rested her head on one side, showing curiosity, and said, 'What does he look like, the man?'

'Oh, he's fearsome, ma'am,' began Mathilda, wringing her hands.

Priscilla snapped at her.

'Do stop wringing your damned hands! Continue.'

'The man is quite old. He's about sixty-five. He is wearing breeches and a waistcoat, both torn to shreds. He's in rags from head to foot. He has thin, dirty, greyish hair, tied untidily in a pony-tail. And that's not the worst of it, ma'am. It's his terrible eyes which struck me. I couldn't look him in the face. They are very pale blue, like an albino's and the pupils are so piercing they could bore holes through stone.'

Priscilla's psychological state was so much improved that she decided to stagger down to the drawing-room to confront the seemingly offensive man aggressively. She remembered the occasion when she had seen him before, while she and Jack were standing near the Thames, feeding the birds.

She found the man sitting in a chair with his feet on a stool, its top covered with a tapestry worked on by her own hand. She was wearing a pink, silk dressing gown, fringed with gold brocade, and her face was white, partly with fear, mainly with rage.

'I've been unfortunate enough to see you once before!' she shouted. 'I don't know who you are and I would thank you to take your muddy feet off my stool this instant.'

The man did so. His action was alarmingly slow and deliberate.

'I demand to know your name. You knocked my maid over when you brutally forced your way into my house. Who are you?'

The man's speech was as slow and deliberate as was his action of removing his feet from the stool. He spoke with a thick, barely comprehensible, Scottish accent.

'My name is Malcolm Robertson. I am the father of George Robertson, the carter,' began the man.

'So what if you are? I've never heard of either of you. Besides that, when you are sitting in someone's drawing-room, it is customary to leap to your feet when that person comes into the room.'

Robertson ignored the rebuke. He was trembling and it was clear he was unwell. He paused while he rolled his albino eyes round the elegant room, occasionally resting them on the *objets d'art*.

'Is that all you've come here to say?' asked Priscilla, who had deliberately remained standing in order to cause Robertson to feel ill at ease.

Robertson said, 'Some time ago, I got took sick with typhoid fever.'

'Please continue. I'm absolutely riveted,' said Priscilla.

'I was in bed for some weeks. It was at the time of the typhoid epidemic. My son, George, looked after me. He saw to me before he left for work in the mornings and nursed me when he came home in the evenings. I used to lean out of my bed and be sick a lot of the time. My son never complained about washing the floor.'

Priscilla assumed this man was no more than a harmless madman and because his reminiscences revolted her she sought comic relief and joked at his expense.

'I don't understand why you were unable to be sick into a bucket, instead of emptying your stomach all over the floor which your son had to wash. He must have found the ordeal absolutely charming, as indeed anyone would, hearing you talk about it.'

'I fear I have a lot more to say to you before I've finished,' said Robertson.

He fixed his eyes on Priscilla and smiled. It was a strange, sinister unearthly smile, revealing only one rotting front tooth, and it made her shudder.

'Once the typhoid fever was over, I still felt very ill. Shaky, weak, low in spirits and dizzy. I was like this for a good three months. The neighbours knew. Sometimes they came to see me when my son was at work.'

Priscilla was bored and exhausted. She rang the bell for Mathilda who scurried into the drawing-room, fearing for her mistress's safety.

'You rang, ma'am.'

'Yes. Would you mind listening to the end of this gentleman's story, please?'

'I'm sorry, ma'am. You know that most times I can refuse you nothing, but I'm not sitting alone in a room with him, not after he barged in here and knocked me down.'

'I understand that, but I must insist that you sit with me until he's gone. He keeps telling me about his health, but I am beginning to suspect that his motives for being here are very much more sinister than I thought at first.'

'You couldn't be more right,' said Robertson, still smiling, adding, not without sarcasm, 'It won't be long before you two ladies find out what really brings me here.'

'Do get on with it. Your presence in this house is offensive to both of us. Finish your story and then get out!' Priscilla shouted.

'I was still feeling very poorly. My son left the house to go to work. He gave me tea and bread first and washed my face and shaved me. He said he'd look in on me again when he came back that evening.'

'I remain fascinated,' said Priscilla. 'Did he look in on you again when he came back that evening, as promised?'

'That is where I am coming to the point,' said Robertson. 'He did not come back. I waited for him for months. He never came back. I haven't seen him since that morning. The only thing that comforts me is feeding the birds by the river. I like routine. I always leave my house at 2.00 o'clock sharp every afternoon. I do so love birds.'

'I'm sorry to hear about your son,' Priscilla forced herself to remark.

'A neighbour of mine saw two men leap out of a hiding place, just as my son was walking down the street, carrying the wee loaf of bread he always had for lunch. The neighbour was looking through the window and was close enough to the two men to give an accurate description of them. Both were fine-looking fellows with wavy black hair and big dark eyes. One of them had a blond streak just above the hairline.

'The neighbour saw these men roughing up my son and knocking him about. They must have seen there was no one out in the street and took advantage of that. The neighbour saw them drag my son away. Word gets round, as you know. My son's body was washed out of the Thames a few days later. The neighbours all got together to help me raise money for a dignified burial. Even after that, I wasn't able to accept that my son was dead.'

Priscilla was sweating and breathing heavily. She summoned the courage to ask the question which tormented her.

'These two men who took your son away, did your neighbour have any idea who they were?'

'Oh, aye. My neighbour knew all right. They were the McArandy brothers. My neighbour often went to the taverns where they were due to play. He thought they were wonderful musicians.'

'Are you sure they were the McArandy brothers?' asked Priscilla.

'I didn't see them. My neighbour is certain. He has a rare gift for recognising faces.'

'Then why didn't your neighbour tell anyone?'

'You know why.'

'Indeed, I do not know why.'

'Because in this neighbourhood there is not a soul who doesn't live in fear of the two brothers and the McArandys always find out if someone is foolish enough to tell on them, no matter how discreetly. And I know that Jack McArandy lives here and word has reached me that you are carrying his wee bairn.'

As on occasions before, when Priscilla heard ill spoken

about the McArandys, she bit her lip and tried to force herself to believe the stories were false.

Then she remembered Jack himself admitting to her that he led another life and had committed acts which he did not wish her to know about. At first, she had thought the brothers had done nothing worse than steal to stay alive.

She recalled Mathilda's words, however vague, about the brothers having been seen swinging a dead body into the Thames, which tallied with Robertson's account of his son's body being found in the water.

Robertson's words when she had first met him, when he came to the house asking for a loaf of bread, crashed through her head so violently that she felt as if she was being stabbed. 'He'll swing one day,' Robertson had said.

Priscilla felt as if she were the victim of multiple stab wounds covering her entire body. She felt she was turning to a block of ice. Her heart thundered against her ribs. The walls of the room started spinning. She screamed until she fainted.

Mathilda brought her round with smelling salts and guided her to a comfortable chair where she recuperated with her head thrown back. The aftermath of the faint made her feel even worse and more nauseated than before but she was able to gather her wits.

She felt like St Sebastian, his body peppered with arrows, and only barely heard Robertson's words, 'Jack McArandy has no idea who I am or where I live but old though I be, I can direct anyone I want to this house.'

She replied, 'I could always tell him your name and, if he is guilty, all he has to do is to return to the street where you live and find you.'

Robertson went a deathly shade of white.

'I've told you the whole truth now, madam, and whose bairn you are bringing into the world. I'll be going, before your fancy fellow comes back.'

98

Robertson felt giddy. He guided himself downstairs, holding the bannister with his heavily-stained hands. He left the house, forgetting to close the door, and staggered into the night. Mathilda hurried downstairs and closed the door before returning to the drawing-room, where she found Priscilla trembling and clutching her stomach.

'Oh, ma'am, you're starting and so early too. You're safe with me. I'll help you upstairs to the bedroom.'

It was an effort to get Priscilla upstairs. Once she was lying on the bed on her back, Mathilda was appalled to see the expression of suicidal despair and terror on her face, which seemed so intense as to diminish the physical pain.

* * *

The contractions had started. There were sufficient intervals between them for her to speak to Mathilda, clutching her arm.

'Help me! I've made the most terrible mistake. I now know for certain who Jack really is. For God's sake, stop me having this child! Drive a knife into my stomach. I can take the pain. All I ask is that you don't let the child live.'

Her empassioned words were interrupted by another contraction. Mathilda prepared a bowl of warm water and fetched some towels from the cupboard in the corridor, together with a woollen baby's shawl which she had made herself.

By the time she returned to the bedroom, Priscilla was having another contraction. Mathilda estimated that she could rush downstairs to arrange for the carriage to travel to The Fife and Drum two miles away to fetch Jack who had said he wished to witness the birth.

The only other person in the house was the elderly cook whose name was Mrs Dodderidge. She had once been Priscilla's nanny. Mrs Dodderidge's personality was not unlike her name. She cooked extremely badly, but Priscilla kept her in her employ because she loved her and had such an undiscerning palate that she was unable to judge the quality of food. Jack, who had eaten rough food for most of his life, never complained about the cooking either.

Mrs Dodderidge frequently burnt what she was cooking because she tended to leave saucepans boiling and frying pans frying while she washed dishes from previous meals. It was not unusual for her to drop piles of plates on the floor.

She was a tiny woman who was only four foot six inches tall. She had rounded shoulders and wore a tight, white cap which she never removed from her head, so no one knew the colour of her hair.

She slept in a small room in the basement of the house and had just managed to get to sleep when Mathilda hammered on her door. Mrs Dodderidge rolled out of bed as Mathilda entered the room.

'Mrs Dodderidge, for God's sake wake up! Miss Priscilla is going into labour. Go straight to the cottage next door to the stables, wake Mr Freshwater up and get him to take the carriage to The Fife and Drum in Midway Lane to fetch Mr McArandy. Hurry!'

Mrs Dodderidge failed to answer but did as she was told.

Freshwater, who like Sarah McArandy, had hailed from a wealthy family which had fallen from grace, was bitter and inclined to be short-tempered. He spoke with a marked educated accent. Many who heard him speak mistook him for a private tutor or a clergyman.

He had never liked Mrs Dodderidge whose clumsiness and scattiness got on his nerves and was furious when she flapped about outside his cottage like a trapped bird, dragging him from deep slumber. He vented his anger on the horses which he lashed with his whip, causing them to change from a gentle canter to a gallop as they passed through the narrow streets.

The few pedèstrians out at 11.00 o'clock that night flung themselves to the sides of the road in an attempt to save their lives.

Freshwater's formal coachman's clothes startled the felons at the crowded Fife and Drum who paid the McArandys exorbitantly and generously each night with stolen money.

Freshwater glanced briefly round the room and failed to find the McArandys. He then mounted a platform to the part of the tavern where the drinking tables were, and found the brothers laughing and joking and drinking ale.

Freshwater found it hard to tell one brother from the other when they were sitting together.

'Mr Jack McArandy?' he said courteously.

'Is something the matter?' he asked.

'It's Miss Priscilla, sir,' he announced loudly. 'She's started to go into labour.'

An occupant of a neighbouring table, who had stolen a jewel case from the back of a stationary coach earlier that day, was stunned on hearing Freshwater's accent and shuddered.

'But that's impossible,' said Jack. 'The nine months aren't up. She's only just over eight months gone.'

'I'm sorry, sir. That is the information I have been given. Mrs Dodderidge came and told me. Mathilda is supervising the delivery and is most anxious that you come at once.'

'All right, I'll come straight away. Ethelred, will you come with me? I'm nervous and I need you there.'

'I'll come,' said Ethelred, 'but on the way, I must tell Sally I won't be going home. She may fret about me.'

'We haven't time to tell Sally, Ethelred,' rasped Jack. 'Can't you tell her tomorrow and say you're sorry then?'

'All right, Jack. I know how frightening it is for any man when a woman gives birth.'

The McArandys scrambled into the back of the carriage.

They had barely sat down when Freshwater cracked his whip and lashed the horses into a gallop, causing the brothers to stumble onto the floor.

When they arrived at the house, Mathilda opened the front door. Jack was alarmed by the fact that she was crying. Ethelred instinctively sensed his fear and was seized by it himself. Jack spoke to Mathilda nervously and very rapidly, without being rude to her, because he associated her with Priscilla and felt affectionately towards her.

'Mathilda, this is my brother, Ethelred,' began Jack. 'I didn't know if you knew I had a brother and I didn't want our identical appearances to startle you.' He added even more hurriedly, 'Is the child born?'

'Gentlemen,' said Mathilda through her tears, 'would you please come up to the drawing-room and sit down.'

The astounded McArandys both felt they were having a bad dream. They did as they were told. They had no wish to argue with a kindly old lady who would have been their mother's age, had she lived.

They were both shaking like autumn leaves, Jack because of his own terror and Ethelred because of his brother's terror. They sat bolt upright on adjacent chairs. Jack was the first to speak.

'Mathilda?' he said.

'Yes, sir.'

'Do you think you could please pour us out a glass of gin?'

'Why, yes, gentlemen.'

She produced one of several stone bottles of gin from the cabinet. She filled up two large glasses and handed them to the McArandys. They both drained them with trembling hands, like water.

'Could you please give us some more of the same amount,' asked Jack.

Mathilda did not reply. She was not looking forward to

saying what she had to say. She filled up the brothers' glasses, followed by a glass for herself.

Jack drained his glass a second time. The gin had made him temporarily bolder.

'Tell us what's happened, Mathilda,' he said.

'At half past eleven, last night, gentlemen, I delivered Miss Priscilla of a son,' she said in a tragic tone.

'A son? She always wanted a son. May I go up and see him?' asked Jack.

'I'm afraid it is not as you imagine, sir. Your son was stillborn!'

'Stillborn? What do you mean?'

Mathilda bowed her head and clasped her hands in front of her and lowered her voice.

'Stillborn means without life, sir. The child was born dead. It was dead before it left its mother's body. As you know, it was born prematurely and it was too weak to survive.'

Jack looked at Ethelred and Ethelred looked at Jack. Both brothers had tears in their eyes.

'Why ever did you let it happen like that?' asked Jack.

'Be fair to me, Mr McArandy. A midwife is not responsible for what goes on inside a woman's womb. She is only responsible for removing the child from her body. Your child was dead before it left its mother's body.'

'What about Priscilla? How is she taking it?' asked Jack suddenly.

Mathilda began to cry again, this time convulsively.

'Oh, sir, this is the most tragic news I have ever had to break to anyone. Miss Priscilla had a dreadful shock before the contractions started. It was too much for her system, and I'm sure that is what started the contractions so early. She died in childbirth, Mr McArandy.'

Jack looked as if he were about to faint.

He said, 'May I go up and see the mother and child?'

'Yes, certainly. I'll come with you if you like.'

'No. There is no need. Perhaps you could give me the bottle of gin to steady the shock.'

'I'll fetch it straight away.'

'Do you want me to come with you, Jack?' asked Ethelred, who was suffering the same intense pain and bereavement as his brother.

'Yes, Ethelred. You must come up with me. Only my other half can help me now.'

As the brothers slowly mounted the staircase leading to the bedroom, Jack called to Mathilda who was hovering outside the drawing-room, trying to pass him the bottle of gin. He reached out for it, opened it and took two more swigs.

'Mathilda?'

'Yes, sir.'

'When Ethelred and I come down I want to hear about the shock Priscilla had before she went into labour.'

'You can trust me, sir. I will tell you. It's something you need to know.'

Jack told Ethelred to go into the bedroom first and then followed him. Priscilla's body was under the covers wrapped in a white, silk nightdress which Jack had given her as a present. Although her face bore the pallor of death, she looked beautiful and serenely asleep. Her dead child was wrapped in a shawl covering its head and her hands were covering it.

At that moment, Jack thought he only needed to call her name to get her to wake up. She looked so alive that he refused to believe she was dead.

Suddenly, he threw himself on top of the dead woman and child and howled with grief, sounding like a pack of wolves. Occasionally, between the intervals of howling, he pressed the bottle of gin to his lips, turned on his back and poured the soothing balm down his throat.

What touched and upset him most of all was the sight of

the new tapestry Priscilla had been working on, which she had left by the side of the bed with the needle threaded as if she were intending to pick it up again at any moment of her choice.

He caressed Priscilla's body all over while his tears became more plentiful, bringing him to the verge of hysteria. He wept onto her dishevelled hair which somehow looked more attractive than when it was meticulously coiffed. He put his hand under her nightgown and fondled her breasts which were as cold as marble. Ethelred stood weeping over his brother's pain. The gin had caused Jack to shed all his manly inhibitions. He turned the noise he was making into words, addressed to the dead woman, uttered with a tragic, heart-broken wail.

'Oh, that I had married you, my sweet and incomparable Priscilla! I did not do so because I feared so much that I would dishonour my pure, beautiful, lady-love. You, my darling, were far too fine and far too good for a rogue like myself, but now that the cruel Reaper has taken you from me, I know from the depth of my heart, which alas still beats when yours does not, that in the sight of heaven, you are my very wife, my own beloved and adorable little doll.'

Jack rolled off the bed and walked towards Ethelred who was standing nearby. Just as they had on finding their dead mother, the brothers put their arms round each other's waists and wept out loud.

Jack said, 'We should go down to the drawing-room now, Ethelred. Mathilda's waiting there and we have to find out what gave Priscilla such a shock before she went into labour.'

Mathilda was there. She had prepared a tray of strong tea for the brothers, who came in and sat in the same chairs they had occupied before. She poured out the tea and waited for them to drink a cup each.

'Tell us about the shock Priscilla had,' said Jack whose speech was slightly slurred.

'When you were at the tavern, a strange old man called at the house. I thought you might have had an accident so I opened the door a few inches to see who was out there. Although he was elderly, the man had the strength to throw open the door and he broke in, knocking me over.'

'Was he in rags, with dirty grey hair tied in a pony-tail?'

'Yes, sir.'

'Did he have pale blue eyes like an albino?'

'Yes, sir.'

'Did he have a thick, nasty accent?'

'He has a Scottish accent.'

'Did he give his name?'

'He said his name was Malcolm Robertson and that he had a son called George Robertson.'

'Oh, GR,' said Ethelred spontaneously.

Jack leapt over and slapped him on the back of the hand.

'Shut up, you damned fool!' he said. 'Go on, Mathilda.'

'He said his son had left for work one morning and never returned. He said a neighbour had seen two men from inside his house dragging him away and treating him roughly. His son's body was found floating in the Thames.'

'Did his neighbour describe either of these men?' asked Jack.

'Yes, he did. He said both men had wavy black hair and dark eyes and that one of them had a blond streak just above his hairline.'

'Do you really think the neighbour, who apparently was inside his house, could see these men in such detail? Besides, it sounds as if this man gave a description of Ethelred and me. I know Robertson because he followed us back here and pestered Priscilla once before. He asked her for a loaf of bread. I certainly don't know anyone called George Robertson.'

'But Mr Ethelred appears to. A moment ago, he called him "GR".'

'I was joking,' said Ethelred. 'I was referring to a boy with the initials GR whom we played with as children.'

'Then why did Mr Jack smack your hand when you mentioned the initials?'

'Because this is a serious discussion and it does not warrant silly interruptions,' said Jack, adding, 'Did Robertson say these things to Priscilla, implying that Ethelred and I were murderers?'

'I am afraid he did. We could neither of us get him out of the house. As soon as he had gone, Miss Priscilla went into labour.

'There was another thing that struck me as being odd. He made a point of saying that he loved birds and that, following his recovery, he left his house at 2.00 o'clock sharp each afternoon to go down to the river and feed them.'

'2.00 o'clock, you say?' said Jack.

'Yes 2.00 o'clock. He said he did this as a daily routine.'

'What sort of mental state was Priscilla in?'

'She was screaming, terrified and hysterical. She actually believed what the old man had told her, and she begged me to push a knife into her stomach to kill the baby.'

Jack whitened.

'What about you, Mathilda? Do you believe those two men were Ethelred and me?'

'No, of course not, sir. I think a rumour was passed around that you had been seen dragging George Robertson* away because someone was jealous of your musical talent. It must have been two other men, two men who knew him, bore a grievance against him and had reason to harm him.'

'I'm sure you're right,' said Jack. 'I wonder who the two men really were and why they were attacking this man, George Robertson. Perhaps he owed them money. Anyway, it was his father who killed the only woman, apart from my mother, whom I really loved.'

'I'm so sorry about the ghastly suffering you have had to

endure. If there is anything I can do I'd be only too glad to do it,' said Mathilda. 'I respect you and think highly of you, sir. I think highly of you both.'

The brothers left the house and went for a long walk that afternoon. Ethelred was worried about Sally and planned to call at the rented room to explain his absence the night before. Jack went to The Fife and Drum, his face wet with tears, and told the people there that his wife had died in childbirth, that his baby had been stillborn and that he would not be in a mentally fit state to work for at least a week.

The people he addressed knew him well and doted on him and Ethelred. They promised to pass his message on and were so saddened by his loss that they collected enough money to provide him with a week's average earnings while he was grieving. He also told them that Ethelred would be coming in every night so that the tavern would not be deprived of music.

* * *

About a week after Priscilla's death, her funeral took place, organised by Jack. Although harrowing, it comforted him to make the arrangements. He felt like creating a work of art in her honour and building something to commemorate his adoration for her, her soft, ivory skin, her doll-like innocence, her sacred gentleness and the idyllic glory of her soul.

A hearse, bedecked with glossy, black plumes, towed by six frisky horses, came to a halt outside the house in Brominster Street. The coffin was already in the hearse, covered by white roses and lilacs, Priscilla's favourite flowers.

It was two miles to the local cemetery, an overgrown, disused, but by no means unromantic place. When Jack and Priscilla had gone for walks together, she had told him how charmed she was by its desolate, barren appearance and by the manner in which it was flanked by evergreen trees, their neatness contrasting with the generalised bleakness, and the mists which rose from the ground on foggy days.

Ethelred and Jack were dressed in black velvet suits, white shirts and black stockings. They walked behind the hearse. Their task was made even more unpleasant by the fact that the horses passed mounds of steaming dung which slurped over their new black shoes and stockings.

Jack did not mind and even found the situation refreshingly humorous. Both brothers put their arms round each other's waists. This was the first time in their lives that their loins were stirred to the core by their mutual brotherly warmth. The feeling was more powerful than Ethelred's love for Sally and was on a par with Jack's love for Priscilla, without a sexual attachment, but equal to the spiritual bond which unites man and woman.

Jack wept convulsively throughout the walk behind the hearse and Ethelred, too, wept for his brother's pain. Their mutual pain was almost transformed to joy, caused by their tight grip on each other and the increasing heat of their bodies.

The weather was foggy and the mist rising from the ground perfected the appearance of the mysterious, strangely beautiful cemetery. As the parson read the burial prayers, while the coffin was being lowered into the grave, Jack sank to his knees and broke down completely. Ethelred took hold of his arm and eased him to his feet.

'Don't be ashamed of your tears, Jack,' he said in a whisper. 'It's not unmanly to cry. It's a sign of strength. It's a sign that you have a soul.'

The two brothers threw their arms round each other and sobbed like hysterical women, while the embarrassed parson, who had just read the prayers while the coffin was lowered, ran his hands through his thinning white hair, formed his right hand into a fist in front of his mouth and let out a genteel little cough.

Within a few weeks, Jack planned for an elaborate carving to be placed on the grave. He did not want a cross. Despite religious trends at the time, he had no belief in a Supreme Being, although Ethelred did. Jack had forced himself to abandon the faith his mother had raised him to adopt. Because of the crimes and murders he had committed, he knew he would go insane were he to allow himself to think he would burn in hell for the rest of eternity. He believed in the after-life only in so far as his reunion with his loved ones was concerned.

He arranged for a sculptor and mason to carve an ivory white statue of Priscilla, modelled on a lifesized portrait of her, her body covered by a skimpy nightdress. He made a special request for her delicate hands, with their long tapering fingers, to be carved palm to palm like a saint at prayer.

The effigy lay on top of the grave on a black marble pedestal. Behind Priscilla's head was a white marble slab engraved with gold Gothic letters. The inscription was short and simple. It read:

> *Here rests Priscilla,*
> *Jack's little doll.*

Until the end of his life Jack visited the grave every after-noon, when it had been customary for him and Priscilla to have their walk. Each day he would lie on top of the marble effigy and passionately kiss Priscilla's half-open mouth. Then he would kneel on the earth and pray out loud to his goddess, convinced she could hear his words. These excursions, together with Ethelred's company at meals, gave him strength and increased his desire to live.

* * *

Sally was in a downcast mood when Ethelred arrived at the rented room. She was dowdily dressed and sitting at the table, leaning forward, supporting her chin with her hand.

Ethelred smiled charmingly at her and pressed some flowers which he had stolen from someone's garden, into her hand.

She accepted them smiling and said, 'I was ever so worried about you last night, Ethelred. I thought you was in trouble. I haven't been able to sleep all night.'

Ethelred took her skinny hands in his.

'I was worried about you, too, because I couldn't get here. Something terrible happened to Jack last night and I had to stay in his house to stop him going mad.'

'What happened?' asked Sally.

'His poor wife died in childbirth and even the baby was born dead.'

'What a horrible thing to happen! I'm ever so sorry. Had you ever met Jack's wife?'

'Only once.'

'What was she like?'

'She was very quiet and shy. It was difficult to talk to her. She was fond of indoor games, sewing and throwing bread to the birds by the river. She was always kind to Jack. He's heartbroken.'

Sally said nothing. She began to put the flowers into a chipped clay vase.

Ethelred continued, 'I'm afraid I'm going to have to stay with Jack for a few days because he's suffering and he needs me. I will call in here every afternoon, though, while he is having the rest he needs so much, as he can't sleep at night. We can do whatever you like. We can go for a walk, go to the fair or just stay here. I'll give you whatever money you need and once Jack is better, I'll come and live here again.'

'That's all right. I don't mind, Ethie, as long as I know you're safe.'

* * *

Ethelred and Jack walked back to Priscilla's house together.

Ethelred said, 'Do you think Mathilda suspects we killed George Robertson?'

'I really don't think so, although it was very stupid of you to mention his initials, implying that you knew him.'

'But I covered myself by saying I knew someone with those initials as a child.'

'Even so, you should think before you speak. Your mouth could get you into serious trouble one day, and me as well.'

A long silence ensued. It was broken by Jack.

'That dreadful man, Malcolm Robertson will have to be punished for killing Priscilla. I think he deserves the death sentence.'

'We know where he lives,' said Ethelred. 'Tinley Street. We saw the house his son walked out of that day. To murder him would not be difficult.'

Jack said, 'The only way to do it is to break into his house at 3.00 o'clock in the morning, stumble about in the dark until we find out where he sleeps and either strangle him or smother him. Remember, you can't afford to be incompetent or slow-witted.'

'Me? Slow-witted?'

'Yes, Ethelred. You are capable of being very slow-witted. Take the time when you visited Priscilla, for instance. Then there was that incident when you referred to GR. You don't know how much damage you are capable of doing, simply because you don't think before you speak and before you act.'

'All right, Jack. I'll make an effort to be less slow-witted.'

'You're going to have to do so if we're to get rid of Malcolm

Robertson. You're the sort of person who would break into his house and shout "Tell us where your bedroom is, Malcolm. We're the McArandy brothers and we've come to murder you. We're not sure yet whether to strangle you or smother you".'

Ethelred found his brother's words witty and had a giggling fit.

'There's nothing funny about it, Ethelred,' said Jack. 'I don't find the idea of going to the gallows particularly comical. If you do, you're obviously a bit simple.'

Although Ethelred was hurt by his brother's jibes, he attributed them to the fact that he was grief-stricken and decided that instead of expecting affability from him in this state he should give him all the affection it was in his power to give and ignore remarks designed to humiliate.

Mathilda had taken a great liking to the McArandys whom she regarded as gentlemen. When she saw them appear at the house at 4.00 p.m. for lunch she was overjoyed to see them because she associated them with Priscilla.

'Come in, gentlemen. Go to the drawing-room and help yourselves to drinks. Mrs Dodderidge, the cook, that is, will have your lunch on the dining-room table in a few minutes.'

'Thank you so much, Mathilda,' said Jack. 'We must ask one thing, though. Please don't call us "gentlemen", or "sir". We'd like you to call us "Ethelred" and "Jack" because we are your friends.'

'God bless you, both! There's one other thing. I do hope Jack will continue to live in the house and Ethelred, I would like you to stay for as long as Jack needs you.'

'Thank you, Mathilda,' said Jack. 'If it's not inconvenient for you, I'd like to sleep in a spare bedroom, as I couldn't bear to sleep in the bed I shared with Priscilla. Ethelred might like that room or, if he doesn't like the idea, perhaps he could sleep in another spare room.'

'What do you think, Ethelred?' asked Mathilda.

'I'd rather sleep in one of the spare rooms if that suits you.'

Jack said, 'It's just as well you don't want to sleep in Priscilla's room tonight. The undertakers won't be coming to collect the bodies until tomorrow.'

Mrs Dodderidge brought the lunch to the table at 4.00 p.m. Lukewarm soup with fish floating in it consisted of the first course. The McArandys were ignorant of the unpleasantness of the dish. The second course was tough, under-cooked beef which most people would have choked to death on, but Ethelred and Jack had strong, sharp teeth and bit into it and swallowed it like sharks. The beef was followed by apple-flavoured cake. This was hard and stale but to the McArandys' undiscerning palates it tasted like nectar.

At the end of dinner, Mrs Dodderidge came in to clear the table. As she picked up the dish bearing the remainder of the cake, her hand slipped and the cake slid to the floor. Mrs Dodderidge hurriedly got onto her hands and knees to pick up the cake. Her head brushed against the table, dislodging the cap which hid her hair. The brothers noticed that her hair colour was grey, streaked with white. In her agitated state she banged her head against the table on rising to her feet and knocked over a jug of water, which caused the two men to have nervous, hysterical giggles.

'Have you been adequately served, gentlemen?' asked Mrs Dodderidge, after she had wiped up the spilled water.

Ethelred and Jack spoke in unison which unnerved her even more.

'Yes, perfectly, thank you, Mrs Dodderidge.'

'Would you care for port or liqueur?'

'No, thank you, very much, Mrs Dodderidge.'

'I trust the beef was not too tough for you.'

'Not at all. It was just how we like it, Mrs Dodderidge.'

As she was getting ready for bed Mrs Dodderidge thought intensively about the McArandys. The manner in which they had spoken in unison, struck her as being strange to the point of being unwholesome. She would have preferred it if they had insulted her. As she had been told they would be staying in the house for a while, she told herself she would have to get used to them.

The brothers were walking towards The Fife and Drum when Jack suddenly remarked, 'Thank God for Mrs Dodderidge! She provides more comic relief than anyone I've ever met in my life.'

'She certainly had me convulsed,' said Ethelred. 'I hope no one asks her to leave because of her extraordinary behaviour.'

'No one can ask her to leave except Mathilda,' said Jack, 'and if that were to happen, we could intervene.'

The brothers parted company. Ethelred continued his journey to the taverns, and because Jack was still mentally unfit to play his violin competently he walked back to Priscilla's house, crying because he knew she would no longer be there to welcome him.

* * *

Within two days, Priscilla's solicitor, Jacob Cohen, arrived at the house. Ethelred and Jack had just finished breakfast which they had downstairs, served by Mrs Dodderidge.

Jacob Cohen was a thin, polite, quietly-spoken man. Mathilda ushered him up to the drawing-room where there was an oak table, used as a writing desk. He was confused when he saw the two identical brothers waiting.

'Might I ask which one of you is Mr Jack McArandy?' asked Cohen gently.

Jack rose to his feet.

'I am,' he said. 'Over there, is my brother, Ethelred.'

'I see. Perhaps you and I could come over to the table. Could we have this discussion in private?'

'Very well. I'll bring two upright chairs for us. Do you want them on the same side of the table or on opposite sides?'

'It would be better to have them on opposite sides. I think,' said Cohen.

Once the chairs had been brought to the table, Jack and Cohen sat down. Cohen produced a legal document and waved it in front of Jack.

'I should think you are wondering what this is. Have you any idea?' asked Cohen.

'No.'

'It is Miss Priscilla's Last Will and Testament, which dates back to eight months ago. I know you have suffered a grievous and irreparable loss, but I do have some good news for you.'

Jack said, 'The only good news for me would be the knowledge that Priscilla had risen from the dead like Lazarus and that she was upstairs waiting for me naked in bed.'

Cohen cleared his throat.

'Mr McArandy, I know that bereavement sometimes makes us flippant in an attempt to shy away from reality, by the use of grim humour, but I must ask you to try to understand what I am saying to you.'

'What good news could there possibly be after this has happened?' asked Jack.

'Mr McArandy, Miss Priscilla has left her house and all her goods and chattels therein to you. She has also left you all her financial assets, amounting to a very considerable sum of money which I will come to later on in this discussion. This will mean that you will be able to live for the rest of your life in luxury and that you will never need to work again.'

Jack was silent. Somehow it seemed unnatural to him never to work when he had worked all his life. Despite his criminal escapades, he thought that a life of complete leisure without the satisfaction of working hard as a musician would be empty and nihilistic.

He decided he would continue to work as before, as well as accepting the fortune offered to him, in case he needed it one day. He hoped he would be able to persuade Ethelred to leave Sally and come and live with him. He loved the camaraderie associated with his profession, and made up his mind that he would tell no one where he lived or how much wealth had come into his hands.

He had some friends at The Fife and Drum who knew he had been living in luxury with a rich lady. Now everyone there knew that she was dead. He told himself he would say, when asked, that he was living in lodgings without saying where and that he would continue to wear the rough clothes he wore even when he lived with Priscilla. Only Ethelred would know his secret.

Later that morning he discussed with Ethelred his meeting with Cohen and confessed that he had received a fortune, having sworn his brother to secrecy.

Suddenly, in a moment of desperation, he said, 'Please, Ethelred, leave Sally and come and live in this house with me. Share my fortune. Now that Priscilla has gone, I couldn't bear to live here alone.'

'I can't, Jack. I hate this house. I hate everything about it. These surroundings are alien to me. Besides, I am in love with Sally. I don't want money. I'd rather live in a tiny room with Sally than have all the money in the world.'

'All right, will you agree to have meals with me?'

'Sally cooks me a meal just after 11.30 every evening. You eat a lot later. I could certainly be with you then. That way I would have two evening meals. That wouldn't be bad, would it?'

'I understand that, but the idea of having lunch without Priscilla would be horrific to me.'

Ethelred said, 'I don't see any problem there either. What time do you have lunch?'

'Half past three.'

'Sally cooks my lunch at 2.00 o'clock. That means I'll be having two lunches and two dinners. I hope it won't make me too stout.'

A surge of grief swept through Jack. He suddenly felt guilty about having told his brother he was slow-witted.

'You're such a dear brother, Ethelred,' he said.

'Keeping you company and helping you become happier is one reason I agreed,' said Ethelred.

'Oh, is there another reason?'

'Mrs Dodderidge gives us so much of the comic relief we need.'

The brothers had lunch at a later time of 5.00 o'clock the following evening. As before, Mrs Dodderidge made Ethelred laugh abandonedly. She brought a tray into the dining-room, on which were jellied eels, leather-hard lamb cutlets and unripe blackberries which were hard.

She was drunk. She walked straight into the wall beyond the table, bumping herself and dropping the tray. The brothers rushed over to help her pick up what had fallen on the floor. Ethelred had the giggles.

'Might I be right in thinking you are a little the worse for wear, Mrs Dodderidge?'

'There's no need to be so rude, Ethelred,' said Jack.

'But we need comic relief. We need laughter.'

'Have as much comic relief and laughter as you wish, gentlemen,' said Mrs Dodderidge, 'but not at my expense. I served as nanny to Miss Priscilla and brought her up. I don't require comic relief after such a tragedy, if you don't mind.'

Jack said, 'We're really sorry, Mrs Dodderidge. We didn't mean to mock you or laugh at you. Ethelred was just trying to be funny to cheer us all up.'

'All right, sir,' said Mrs Dodderidge. She picked up the fallen food and put it on the table where the plates were. 'I may only be a humble cook but that doesn't exempt me from feelings of grief.'

'As I say, I can't apologise enough,' said Jack. 'Ethelred, say you're sorry, too.'

'I'm so sorry, Mrs Dodderidge,' said Ethelred. 'If you want the truth, I'm very much the worse for wear myself. I was rude to you. Will you forgive me?'

Mrs Dodderidge shifted her weight from one foot to the other, which was something she did when she was ill at ease. The brothers noticed her face was wet with tears. She appeared not to have accepted either of their apologies.

'I hope you enjoy your lunch. I will come back later to collect the plates.'

After she had gone the brothers started to shovel the jellied eels into their mouths.

'You're not to make any more fun of Mrs Dodderidge, Ethelred,' said Jack.

'All right, Jack. I won't. I was only trying to make you laugh. Incidentally, what are you going to do with all that money?'

'Keep it until I really need it, or until you need it.'

'But we could give up our work. We could travel abroad.'

'I was born and bred in London and I'll die in London,' said Jack. 'I have no wish to go abroad. Nor do I wish to stop working. The money, which we can share, will stop us needing to commit robberies. Why don't you buy Sally some new clothes?'

'Have you seen her recently? Does she need new clothes?'

'I saw her in the street yesterday. She looked like a beggar.'

Ethelred was hurt.

'Give me some money to buy her a trousseau of clothes, then,' he said in a hoarse whisper.

Jack produced £2 from his pocket.

'Take this and smarten her up,' he said.

Within a week, Sally changed from looking like a penniless waif to an elegant lady. She did not know how Ethelred had obtained the money, but she appeared as appreciative as a dog greeting its master on his return home.

* * *

The McArandys went for another walk the following day. Jack was depressed and in a brooding mood.

He said, 'We've got to do something about that louse, Malcolm Robertson, and the sooner the better. He's not going to get away with killing Priscilla and our child. Apart from Mother, she was the only woman I loved and worshipped to distraction and her memory will be sacred to me until I die. Other than dirt-cheap, degraded whores, I shall never take a woman to my bed again.'

'Trust me my big brother,' said Ethelred. 'That insect must be murdered and I will help you. Have you thought of a plan of action?'

'I'm sure I remember where his house in Tinley Street is and so do you. We saw his son leave the house that morning when we took him away. I suggest we cover our faces with handkerchiefs to be especially cautious and that we break into the house at 3.00 o'clock tomorrow morning. There won't be a soul about then.

'I'll go to my house and find two handkerchiefs. I'll meet you outside The Fife and Drum. It won't be midnight by the time you come out, which means we'll have a lot of time to kill before we arrive at Tinley Street at 3.00 o'clock in the morning. We won't go anywhere near Tinley Street until the right time. It won't take us too long to get there as it's not far from the tavern.

'Once we get to Tinley Street, we'll wrench open Robertson's front door. I'll bring a glass vase with a candle in it. Priscilla kept a lot of those in the house. We will go through the house until we find his room. It's likely he'll be asleep. If he isn't and jumps out of bed to escape, we'll just have to chase him until we catch him. Then we'll kill him.

'The only thing I'm worried about is you losing you head and making a noise. Also, your reactions are quite slow when things don't go as planned.'

'I won't make a noise, Jack,' said Ethelred.

The brothers sauntered to Tinley Street, via a particularly rough area where ragged prostitutes were huddled dejectedly in broken-down doorways, hungrily drinking gin to forget their hopeless and wretched existence.

The McArandys arrived at Tinley Street at 2.55 a.m. The street was even filthier than it had been on their last murderous visit. Piles of rotting food were strewn across the street, making carts and even wagons pulled by tradesmen unable to pass. Chunks of meat, which had gone off, stank of decomposing bodies. The McArandys retched but were able to prevent themselves from being sick.

They both thought of their mother's cleanliness and their hatred for Robertson intensified. Two well-fed rats scuttled around their feet. They both had a terror of rats, which they associated with neglectful hygiene and decay, and shuddered.

They reached the end of Tinley Street and were glad to be wearing their handkerchiefs which diminished the vile smell. When they communicated, they spoke in hushed whispers.

'That's Robertson's house,' said Ethelred, pointing to a dilapidated, pale-stoned house covered in cracks and grime.

'Hold the candle, Ethelred. I'll open the front door,' said Jack.

He only had to lean on the door to get it to open. Ethelred followed him into the house, carrying the candle. Their task was easy. They heard the sound of hoarse snoring coming from a ground-floor room. When they went in, they saw the embers of a log fire and a poker lying nearby. They walked towards the bed which, surprisingly, had a clean, white, lace counterpane covering it. They noticed two blankets protruding from underneath, pulled up above the sleeper's shoulders. They were astounded by the cleanliness of the sleeper's bed, in contrast to the repulsively dirty street in which he lived.

They went closer to the bed. The sleeper had thin, greyish hair and was sleeping face downwards.

Ethelred held the candle close to the man's head.

'That's Robertson, isn't it, Jack?' he mouthed.

'It couldn't be anyone else. Look at the hair colour. Besides, this is his house. I'm going to strike now. Hold the candle steady and keep it above his head.'

Jack went to the fireplace and picked up the poker which he carried over to the sleeper, while Ethelred continued to hold the candle, his hands shaking.

Jack said, 'Don't let your hands shake, Ethelred. It's a sign of fear and of not being in command of a situation. To do what we're doing needs nerves of steel. If you had nerves of steel your hands would not be shaking.'

Jack bent over the man and struck him on the back of the head ten times, killing him after the first stroke.

He said, 'Keep holding the candle while I turn him over, Ethelred. There won't be any injuries to his face, which means that anyone suspicious of his disappearance, who decides to see if he is in the house, would think he had died in his sleep.'

Jack turned the dead man's body over. Ethelred had never met Robertson and was curious to see what his face looked like. He held the candle close.

'There's no bleeding or sign of injury on his face,' he said. 'We've done well tonight.'

Jack was tired and drowsy. He leant over to examine Robertson's face to give himself the satisfaction that he had avenged his beloved Priscilla's honour. Suddenly his eyes widened and his face whitened. He told himself that what he suspected was probably groundless, but he had an obsessive urge to prove it.

He opened one of the dead man's eyes.

'Bring the candle close to the eyes, Ethelred,' he snapped.

'What for?'

'Never mind what for! Just do as I say.'

As Ethelred held the candle two inches away from the dead man's eyes, Jack came out in a cold sweat.

'What's the matter, Jack?'

'Sweet Christ!' shouted Jack. 'We've killed the wrong man. Robertson has albino eyes. This man's eyes are brown.'

'You mean we've killed an innocent man, a man who's never harmed us?' gasped Ethelred.

'Yes. That is exactly what we've done. It's too late now. Either the man we killed is a friend or relative of Robertson's who was invited to stay, perhaps in his absence, or we mistook this house for his. Robertson is still alive, I'm afraid. I'm not giving in. I'm still going to kill him with your help. I've got some idea how I'm going to find out where his house actually is, but I'll tell you tomorrow when we go for a walk after breakfast. The main thing is to get out of here and get out fast. I don't know when the sun rises, but we can't afford to be seen in this area when dawn comes. Come on. Don't dawdle. We've got to get out of this house and out of this area now. By now, I don't mean in ten minutes' time, I mean immediately.'

Ethelred was so shocked on learning that he had participated in the killing of an innocent man, that he stood motionless by the bed, his feet glued to the floor.

Jack was exasperated. He grabbed him roughly by the scruff of the neck and dragged him from the room, outside into the street. He closed the front door quietly behind him.

'We're at the end of Tinley Street, now,' he said. 'We have only about twenty yards to go and we'll be in a wooded area. It means a longer walk but it's the safest way out.'

Jack arrived at his house at about 5.00 o'clock in the morning. He let himself in with his key. No one in the house had woken. Frustrated and deeply depressed, he went quietly to the spare bedroom he had chosen and got into bed without removing his clothes. He wished Ethelred were still staying with him and felt angry with Sally for monopolising him.

*　*　*

Ethelred let himself into the rented room he shared with Sally at about 4.30 a.m. Sally had slept badly the night before and had taken laudanum the following night to avoid insomnia.

She had taken a fractionally higher dose than her apothecary had advised, and was sleeping deeply by the time Ethelred returned. When she woke at 9.00 o'clock in the morning, she was under the impression that she had fallen asleep before Ethelred was due back from the taverns and remained in ignorance of his prolonged absence.

When Ethelred woke at 8.00 a.m., he shaved, splashed his body all over with water, combed his hair and put on clean clothes. He waited for Sally to wake up and brought her a mug of tea, accompanied by bread and honey.

'You're so good to me, Ethie,' she said. 'Do you know that I've realised I can't sleep without laudanum? Is it a habit-forming medicine? I seem to need more and more and if I don't have any I don't get to sleep at all.'

Ethelred knew that Jack would need him to assist in Robertson's murder that night. He saw the logic of acting before the innocent man's body was found. He knew that once this happened, the inhabitants of Tinley Street would become suspicious and might even decide to take it in turns to sit up all night, their faces pressed to their windows, to ensure that no shady-looking characters loitered in the street at any time during the night.

Ethelred's thoughts turned to Sally's question. It was imperative that she should have laudanum again the following night, in an even higher dose than before. If she found out that he was out for several hours during the night once he was living with her again, instead of with Jack, there was a risk that she might make an unpleasant scene.

'What are you thinking about, Ethie?' asked Sally.

'I was thinking about your question. I have been told that laudanum is not a habit-forming drug and that you can take it whenever you like, particularly to sleep. You mustn't take too heavy a dose, though, because it might make you feel rather ill. How many sprinkles did you take last night?'

'Four.'

'That's nothing. Tonight, you can take at least six. It won't harm you. It's not wise to take it indefinitely, though. Once your sleep is restored, you'll be able to stop it altogether.'

'All right, Ethie, I'll take six sprinkles tonight. You know how I always trust your advice.'

Ethelred and Jack went for their constitutional walk after breakfast served by Mrs Dodderidge, when they discussed the plan for killing Malcolm Robertson.

Jack said, 'I now know how I can find out which of the houses in Tinley Street he lives in. You're going to laugh but I'm absolutely serious.

'We have information that Robertson leaves his house at 2.00 o'clock in the afternoon to go to the banks of the Thames to feed the birds. I've asked Mrs Dodderidge to give us a light meal promptly at mid-day, I'm going to Tinley Street alone and in disguise.'

He paused to wait for a reaction from Ethelred who said, 'Disguised as what? A juggling bear?'

'No. A whore,' said Jack.

'W-h-a-a-t?'

'I said as a whore. I'm going to get drunk first to drown my grief a little. Then I'm going to wear Priscilla's pink taffeta maternity dress which she wore only a week before she died. It's big enough to fit my heavy build. I'll wear her white lace shawl round my shoulders. I'll wear one of her wigs, the ash-blonde one which is long with ringlets. Then I'll paint my face with the cosmetics she kept in her vanity case. I'll put on her white lace-up boots, which will be too small, but that is no matter.'

Jack's words tailed off. He felt a choking sensation in his throat and feared he was about to cry. He did not wish to do this in front of Ethelred again as he knew he looked up to him as his resilient, tougher brother. He made a slight sobbing noise which he managed to turn into an artificial laugh. Ethelred had hysterical giggles and, once Jack had controlled himself, he too had the giggles.

Jack said, 'Priscilla gave me a beautiful travelling bag for my birthday on January 2nd. It seems a century ago. The tapestry on the back and front of the bag was worked on lovingly by her own hands. It took her two months to finish it.'

Suddenly, he broke down.

'Oh, Christ, Ethelred, I loved that woman so!' he shouted and threw his arms round his brother and sobbed on his shoulder. 'I'm supposed to be tough and protective towards you, my little brother, and yet I am weeping on your shoulder like a lovesick maid.'

'It doesn't matter, Jack. Some say it's a sign of strength for a man to cry.'

'I used to see Priscilla working on the travelling bag. She always put out her delicate pink tongue in concentration while she pulled the wool through the holes. On the front of the bag, there is what she called a seventeenth-century design, showing a wistful-looking woman standing playing the harpsichord. It was the floor which caught my eye. It was made up of black and white squares like a chessboard. She always told me how much she liked seventeenth-century things.

'On the back of the bag is a picture of country people skating on a lake. It helps me to talk about this in such detail, Ethelred. Somehow I associate that bag with good luck. That is why I'm going to use it this afternoon.

'After we've eaten we'll leave the house. I'll wear my ordinary clothes. I will put Priscilla's dress, white shawl, wig, vanity case and lace-up boots in the bag. As yet you have never shown me where you live. We will go to your room, where I will change and paint my face like a coarse street woman. Perhaps I could do this outside your room because

Sally probably remembers that night I bedded her and it would embarrass us both if she saw me.'

Ethelred didn't like the idea of his brother seeing where his room was and the notion of his meeting Sally again was an anathema to him.

He said, 'All right, Jack. I feel uneasy because of Sally, but I am your brother and nothing will stop me avenging you.'

Jack was astounded when Ethelred showed him where he lived. He expected his brother's room to be part of a building. Instead, it was a shed built with rotting wood, surrounded by a small patch of land covered with shrubs and bushes. He decided not to mention his astonishment to Ethelred for fear of hurting him.

He said, 'This is quite a quiet, pleasant place to live in and to think I've never been here before. I'll go to the back of the shed and change there.'

'It's not a shed, Jack, it's a room.'

'Shed or room, call it what you will. I haven't much time. Come round to the back and make sure no one's about.'

Jack changed into his woman's clothes with brisk, business-like speed to hide his emotion. He noticed Priscilla's perfumed odour on the dress as he pulled it over his head. He bit his tongue to control himself and tied the white lace shawl round his neck to hide his bare chest.

He left the boots, three sizes too small for him, until last. As Ethelred held the vanity case for him to see his reflection in the mirror beneath the lid, he plastered three layers of pasty, flesh-coloured cream onto his face, as well as adding blusher to his cheeks.

He put a thin brush into a bottle containing an ink-black solution and painted it onto his eyelashes and eyelids. As he did so, he wondered how any woman could force herself to have such close contact with her eyes in the interests of vanity. He felt his eyes fill with tears and bit his tongue again, to stop the eye make-up being disturbed.

He dipped the brush into the ink-black solution a second time and painted a heart-shaped black mark on his right cheek and another identical mark on his chin. When the brazen whore's face stared back at him from the mirror, his hatred for loose women, coupled with his all-enveloping love of Priscilla's memory, intensified with a passion so virulent and vehement that it frightened him.

He then forced the boots onto his feet, which took him ten minutes, and even after that amount of time, he had to fiddle with the intricate laces covering at least a foot of stiff leather. He had to sit on the ground to lace up the boots. Ethelred pulled him to his feet.

As Jack was putting his waistcoat, shirt, breeches and shoes into the travelling bag, Ethelred pointed at him and let out a guffaw, followed by prolonged maniacal laughter. Sally had been in the shed, sleeping, but was woken by the noise Ethelred was making. She rushed outside and followed the sound to the back of the shed.

'Oo's that woman with you, Ethelred? What do you think you're doing? What's 'er name?'

'Come a bit closer, Sally, and you'll see,' replied Ethelred. 'It's not a woman. It's a man dressed up as a woman.'

'What's 'ee doing 'ere?'

'He's an actor I met in The Fife and Drum. His name's Harold. He's got to appear in a play later this afternoon and I've been helping him get dressed.'

'Oh, I see. Why didn't you bring him inside? Why all this sneaking about, going to the back?'

'I knew you were resting, Sally. You were furious with me once when I disturbed your sleep. A man can never win, can he?'

Sally was not graced with a sense of humour but she laughed at Ethelred's attempt at merriment.

'Come on inside, both of you. I'll brew up some tea.'

'You're a good girl, Sally, but Harold can't stay. He's got to walk all the way to the theatre in tight ladies' boots which are going to slow him down. I'll stay, though.'

Jack briefly shook hands with Sally, but didn't speak in case she recognised his voice. Instead, he bared his even white teeth in a radiant smile.

Although he had been to Tinley Street more than once, Jack failed to judge the distance to be covered in agonising women's boots, which made him feel as if his feet were being crushed on the rack. He went into a doorway and took them off, a process which was almost as difficult as putting them on.

Just before he turned into Tinley Street, he put them on once more, relieved because the physical pain was temporarily helping to obliterate his grief and was preventing him from breaking down again.

It was the first time in his life that physical pain was as much a relief to him as the flask of gin which he kept hidden under the lace shawl. He took a few swigs and almost forgot his aching feet. He did a theatrical affectation of a woman's walk and moved on to the part of Tinley Street which was closest to the wooded area near where Robertson lived.

He looked at his watch which he wore on a chain round his neck. The time was 1.45 p.m. Priscilla had given him the watch. He felt himself becoming sentimental again and bit his tongue until it bled.

He copied a prostitute's stance, standing with one leg slightly bent and the other straight. He felt the crispy material of the dress and crunched it in his right hand, holding the flask of gin in his left. Occasionally he flicked the material of the dress in different directions, throwing back his head like a seductive street female and patted the ringlets of his wig.

He waited until 2.00 p.m. by which time he had perfected his flouncing, feminine gestures and found they came so naturally to him after practice that he was nervous he might make them once he was wearing his own clothes. He added to his performance by lifting the two sponges which simulated breasts, with slow, rhythmical movements.

By 2.15 p.m., Robertson still had not left his house. Jack's confidence began to dwindle and the pain in his feet was worse. He told himself he had plenty of time and would wait all afternoon if necessary.

The thought crossed his mind that the Scotsman might be ill and he sank into a depression. He did not like the idea of repeating the exercise the following day, particularly as the chances of the body of the man he had killed being found were increasing, not by the day but by the hour.

He knew that for Priscilla's sake he had to discipline himself and have nerves of steel. So vehemently did he believe in defending her honour that he told himself he must be prepared to end his life on the gallows. Even if he were caught tracking down and killing Robertson, his pain, discomfort, risk factor and loss of masculine dignity, would be in the interests of the duty he had once owed to his mother and now owed to Priscilla.

2.30 came. There was still no sign of Robertson. If, as he had been told, he left his house routinely at 2.00 o'clock to feed the birds, the explanation for his absence would either be that the man had already left the house before he arrived or that an illness had prevented him leaving at all.

He took two more swigs of gin, which anaesthetised his brain, and caused him no longer to care whether he avenged Priscilla's honour or not.

By the time it was 2.45 p.m. he told himself he would wait another 15 minutes and arrange with Ethelred to kill the man another time. He felt disappointed and defeated. He was about to leave the street via the wooded area when the door of one of the houses opened slowly.

The first thing he saw was a man's hand holding the door

as if he were afraid to come into the street. The hand was extremely elderly and its fingers were deformed with arthritis. As the door opened further, Jack saw the man coming out of the house, closing the door behind him. In his left hand he was holding a broken loaf of bread.

Jack's feelings of hope had returned. He spoke to himself out loud, as he fondled the watch Priscilla had given him.

'This is the house, Priscilla. This is it, Mother.'

He watched the man walk down the street towards him, his eyes on the ground to prevent him falling over. He seemed drunk. As he came closer Jack noticed his thin, grey hair and pony tail.

He knew the man had seen him, as he suddenly raised his head and observed him with his albino eyes. He was sure the man was Robertson. Indeed, there was not a single facial feature which did not belong to Robertson.

Robertson was now only two feet away from him. It was clear he was fascinated by his appearance, although he saw the tall, elegantly dressed prostitute as a total stranger.

Jack patted his ringlets, flicked the material of his dress and coquettishly lifted his artificial breasts. Because he was a professional musician, he was capable of mimicking any accent and even able to talk convincingly like a woman. He feared Robertson was too doddery, too drunk and too shy to open a conversation with a prostitute. He needed to hear Robertson speak, so that his thick Scottish accent could be confirmed.

Jack said, 'Fancy a roll in the hay, good sir? All I ask for is a little piece of your bread for my services.'

'You canna have any of my bread,' Robertson replied, his Scottish accent even thicker due to his drunkenness. 'I'm going to the river to feed it to the wee birds.'

'What a kind man you must be! Do you do that every day?'

'Every day at 2.00 o'clock, I go to feed the birds, the poor wee things. I was so tired today I got up later than usual.'

131

'Do you have a family?'

'No. I live alone. They've all gone. Even my son's gone. Two cruel men came and dragged him away. His body was found in the Thames. The only comfort I have is that his body was food for the poor, wee birds.'

Jack continued to pat his ringlets.

'I'm so sorry to hear it, sir. Can I not offer you a little comfort before you go to the river? We need only go back to your house.'

'I don't seek that kind of comfort,' replied Robertson angrily. 'I'm too old for kissin' and flirtin'. Take a wee word of advice from me. You'll nae get any trade in a street like this. The people living here are too poor to go buying a woman.'

Jack looked about him. He and Robertson were the only people in the street. He could have strangled the man there and then, without having to make another visit. Although there was no one about, the chances that curious neighbours could be peering out of windows, were far from remote.

He said, 'I'll go somewhere else then, if here's no good. Thank you for letting me know. I'm only new to the trade. I hope there'll be plenty of birds for you to feed. Fare you well.'

'Good afternoon to 'ee and good luck,' said Robertson.

Jack stood motionless while Robertson walked down the street with a shambling, shuffling gait.

Jack looked closely at his house. Like all the other houses, Robertson's house had shabby, dirty, cracked outside walls. His were of dour, dark grey. The front door had no particular colour. It had a prominent crack from top to bottom and its many layers of paint, each of a different shade, were peeling.

Jack noticed a tiny upturned brass horseshoe on the door. Now that the moon would be full again that night, to enable him and Ethelred to find their way, the killing of Robertson without detection was guaranteed, just as the sun was guaranteed to rise the following dawn.

He walked as far as the wooded area and removed the boots which had cut into his feet and made them bleed. He was so overjoyed that he threw them in the air and drank the remainder of his gin.

'By dawn tomorrow, you will be avenged, my beloved little doll!' he said out loud.

*   *   *

It was about 5.00 p.m. by the time Jack arrived at the shed Ethelred liked to refer to as his 'room'. Sally had developed a fever and was asleep. Jack peered through the window and saw his brother sitting on a chair, bending over, looking suspiciously at the mattress on which she lay. Whenever she was unwell he always thought she was iller than she actually was.

The window was ajar. Jack put his hand through it to attract his brother's attention. Ethelred left the shed to speak to him. So close were the brothers that each often knew what the other was thinking, something which had intensified since Priscilla's death. Jack knew that Ethelred thought Sally was seriously ill and he also knew, because of her very connection with Ethelred, that there was little the matter with her.

He said, 'She's all right, little brother. It's only an infection going round. I had it the other day. So did Mrs Dodderidge. It doesn't last longer than two days.'

'How do you *know*, Jack?'

'I usually know what's wrong with anyone close to you, whether I like them or not. I also know on most occasions how you think and how you feel. It's tonight, Ethelred. The man lives in the house with the horseshoe on the door, not the one next to it, which is where the man we killed lived. Robertson's house has filthy, dark grey walls, a door with a crack down the middle and an upside-down horseshoe on it. This is the time to strike, while the moon is still full.'

Ethelred looked down at the weeds and stubbled grass. He said nothing.

'I know what you're thinking, little brother.'

'What am I thinking?'

'You're terrified of being away for a good part of the night and leaving Sally alone, because you think she'll die, don't you?'

'Yes.'

'I told you before and I'll tell you again. Sally is not very ill and she will not die in the night. Not only that, I want my bag so that I can change into proper clothes.'

Ethelred took Jack behind the shed and gave him his bag. He took off the shawl and dress with an air of reverence, like a man of the cloth blessing his vestments. Then he removed the wig and put the boots he had been carrying into the bag. He pulled out his own clothes and dragged them onto his exhausted body.

Priscilla carried a solution in her vanity case for removing make-up, accompanied by a sponge. Jack scrubbed the paint from his face and hugged Ethelred.

'I'm going home for a rest,' he said. 'I will pick you up at The Fife and Drum at half past eleven. We'll have a drink first. Then we'll go straight to Tinley Street. Once all this is over, I'll be only too happy to get back to work.'

'Sally will be all right, won't she, Jack?'

'Yes, little Ethelred, she'll be all right.'

'There's something else worrying me,' said Ethelred.

'I know.'

'You know? Tell me, then.'

'You are having doubts about tonight. You are thinking how wrong it is to have killed a frail, defenceless old man last night and to kill another equally frail defenceless old man again tonight.'

'Yes, that's what I was thinking. Isn't it wrong to murder a party too weak to hit back, when he is sleeping?'

'No, little brother. It's not wrong. Last night was an accident. Robertson may be old and frail but the tongue in his head is healthy, agile and dangerous. Not only has it ruined my happiness and chances of raising a family, it could injure other people as well.

'You could ask why we can't prize open his mouth and cut it out like a canker and still let him live to feed the birds. Of course, we can't do that. We don't want him to suffer more than is necessary. If we simply take his life, his tongue will stop working like the rest of his body.

'Defenceless though he may be, you've got to understand this is a matter of honour. If we were killing a five-year-old child, it would be different. A five-year-old child is innocent and can do no evil. Robertson can and does do evil. Can you not understand that, Ethelred?'

Ethelred thought for a while.

'After hearing you explain it, I think I can understand it, Jack,' he said. 'I just wish the man was younger and could be allowed to put up a fairer fight.'

'You're talking soft, little brother. You're talking like a fool. There are times when honour cannot be defended fairly. To me, honour is a supreme being. It governs my thoughts, my actions and my judgement. We must learn to sacrifice our freedom to live, for it. We must even be prepared to sin for it. Wrong sometimes has to be done in the interest of right. If anything ever happened to you, I'd avenge you too and hang for it on Tyburn Tree and I'd die with a smile.'

Ethelred had been looking his brother in the eye throughout his lengthy speech and was hypnotised by his words.

'Everything you say is right, Jack,' he said, like one who had been brainwashed. 'I won't let you down tonight and because it is something personal to you, I, too, am prepared to hang on Tyburn Tree and I too will die with a smile.'

Jack ruffled his brother's hair and playfully tweaked his

blond streak. He looked at the watch Priscilla had given him. It was 5.00 p.m.

'Good lad. Dear sweet lad. Let's go and have something to eat, and another thing.'

'What, Jack?'

'Don't you dare make mockery of poor old Mrs Dodderidge. I'll give you a good hiding if you do. She's never done anyone any harm. She was Priscilla's nanny once. She brought her up. This means Mrs Dodderidge was effectively her mother. That why I demand that you respect her.'

'I'm not going to mock Mrs Dodderidge, Jack. I did say I wouldn't before,' said Ethelred in an exasperated tone.

'Kindly see to it that you don't!'

Mrs Dodderidge gave the McArandys beef soup, cold chicken and cheese. As was always the case, the food was unpleasant and unappetising, but they were both satisfied, noticing nothing wrong with it.

They stayed in The Fife and Drum until 1.00 a.m. drinking tankards of ale, followed by gin, to give themselves the courage to return to Tinley Street at 3.00 o'clock.

Once they had left the tavern, they wandered the streets aimlessly on their way to Tinley Street, sharing their thoughts and emotions. They were able to do this without speaking and without touching. Their bond had deepened so much that there were times when their conversations were lengthy and unspoken.

They reached Tinley Street just before 3.00 a.m. For some reason they saw fewer starving, gin-swigging prostitutes sitting in doorways than the night before. They came to the unspoken conclusion that these women had found a string of clients to occupy them throughout the night.

They put on their masks. Jack handed the glass vase from his house, containing the candle, to Ethelred so that he could complete the work while Ethelred provided the light.

They walked on separate sides of the road, illuminated by the full moon, until they came to Robertson's house. They looked about them to make sure there were no witnesses. Ethelred held the candle to the front door. Jack checked twice that there was a horseshoe on the top of the door.

He pushed hard against it and, like the door he had opened the night before, it gave way easily. He entered the house with Ethelred following him, holding the candle.

They had no idea which room Robertson was occupying and only assumed that he was alone in the house. They decided to search each room.

The first room they entered was on the ground floor to the left of the door. They had the impression that it had not been used for a considerably long time. The smell in the room was insupportable and powerful. The McArandys were relieved to be wearing their masks, which diminished the smell but did not obliterate it.

Ethelred held the candle above his head, enabling all the objects in the room to come into focus. Close to the door was an unemptied chamber-pot covered with cobwebs and encircled by buzzing insects.

Nearby, was a large bowl of onions which had once been boiled, but had dried and left a dark brown stain around the inside of the bowl. It was a common practice at that time to boil onions in a bowl and inhale their fragrance to treat colds.

On two tall stools near the bowl was a pair of birdcages. One of these contained the skeleton of a small bird which could once have been a magpie. In the other cage, was the skeleton of a pigeon.

On the floor was an unframed miniature oil painting of a red-haired boy, aged about fifteen. The brothers noticed his bone structure and imagined him with a full red beard. They thought this was the face of George Robertson whose body they had thrown into the Thames.

Ethelred shone the candle onto some dusty shelves by the

wall. On one of the shelves were a few loose wrinkled potatoes with secondaries growing out of them like cancers. The brothers were revolted but fascinated to see ants burrowing into them and small worms crawling out of them, as if chased out by the ants.

On another shelf, they noticed a few loaves of bread, eaten into by mildew, unfit, even for the starving. Perhaps, this was the bread which Robertson fed to the birds.

Nearby, lay a dusty Bible, a burnt-out candlestick and a half-full stone bottle of gin.

Jack said, 'The man's filthy. No wonder he always looks ill. His house is full of worms and germs.'

They crossed the tiny hallway to the room to the right of the front door. Onto the wall were nailed three puckered oil paintings of men in kilts. The paintings, like the objects in the other room, were covered in dust.

A small rectangular wooden table stood in the centre of the room, dwarfed by two tall wooden stools. There were rotten apple and pear skins on the table, as well as a fresh loaf of bread.

The brothers went up the creaking stairs, which had holes in, caused by rotting wood on each step, occasionally trapping the heels of their shoes. They held onto the bannisters with both hands to prevent themselves from stumbling, but the bannisters were loose and nearly came away in their hands.

They had never seen the interior of such a neglected, unhygienic house as this before and were so intrigued that they treated it as a museum. Even their friends on the wharf lived in cleaner conditions than Robertson.

They turned left at the top of the stairs into a bedroom which was unoccupied. They saw an uncovered mattress and pillow on a narrow, wooden bed on which two coarse blankets were bundled together in a ball.

On the floor was a bowl filled with soapy water. It had been there for many months. There was a thick, grey film on top of the water and layers of grime on the sides of the bowl.

There was a cracked china bowl under the bed. Although it had been emptied, it had traces of vomit stuck to its bottom. The brothers were nauseated but were able to hold their bile. Also, on the floor, was an ancient, well-thumbed book about Scottish history.

'Can you imagine Mother allowing our home to get into this fearsome state?' said Ethelred, his voice inadvertently raised in horror.

'For God's sake keep your voice down, you damned fool!' said Jack in a hoarse whisper. 'The man we're looking for is probably in the next room. Now, we'll have to sit in here in silence for ten minutes while he overcomes his suspicions that there is someone in his filthy, disgusting house.'

Robertson's room was adjacent to the empty one. The brothers took their shoes off and went in. Robertson was lying on an unsheeted mattress in his day clothes. His body was partially covered by a foul-smelling brown blanket. He was lying on his back and breathing in short wheezy gasps.

On his small bedside table were two candles, one still lit, the other burnt out. There was a piece of charcoal near the candles, accompanied by a birdcage, containing two stuffed robins and a stuffed thrush.

The floor was covered with many immaculately presented drawings of gulls, terns, magpies, pigeons, thrushes and swallows. There was another pile of drawings, over a foot high in the corner.

In another corner was a metal bucket half-filled with clear water and a chamberpot. When the brothers looked under the bed, they found 20 canvas bags of coins, comprising Robertson's life savings.

They advanced towards the bed, speaking only in hushed whispers.

Ethelred said, 'I'm holding the candle to his face so that you can be sure you're killing the right man.'

'Shut up! I can see it's the right man! He's stirring. Throw yourself onto his body. Hurry!'

Ethelred did as he was told. Jack wrenched the heavily-stained pillow from under Robertson's head and rammed it onto his face, throwing his entire weight onto it.

Robertson's legs made violent, involuntary kicking movements of such phenomenal power that Ethelred was covered in bruises as he lay on top of him.

Eventually, the kicking stopped.

'All right, Ethelred. You can get off now. He's dead.'

Ethelred held the candle over Robertson's face. 'Shall I close his eyes, Jack?'

'Do so if you want. You can even cross his hands for all I care. Help me lift his body. We're putting him under the bed with his earnings. Then I'm going to cover him with the blanket. That way, it will take a long time to find him. If a neighbour comes to the house, he'll just think he's gone away. We'd better check the rest of the house. We'd be in a lot of trouble if the man had someone staying. We'd have to kill that person as well and that would really be exhausting.'

As the McArandys left the room, they saw something they had not noticed earlier. A life-sized crucifix covered one of the walls and beneath it was a broken cartwheel, a token of the Robertson family's trade for generations. George Robertson had been a carter and so had his father and ancestors before him.

'I certainly had no idea the man was so devout,' said Jack. 'Come on, we'll check the house. Besides, I want to go to bed.'

The brothers searched the top floor and found there were no more rooms. They went downstairs cautiously because of the dangerous staircase. The two rooms they had seen already were the only rooms on the ground floor. They opened the back door to make sure it didn't lead to another room. All they found was a patch of overgrown grass on which lay the skeleton of a spaniel puppy.

'The man was never very kind to animals, was he?' said Ethelred.

'I don't think he was kind to anything or anyone. Hurry up. We're leaving here at different times. You'd better go first because you'll have Sally fussing after you. Take the wooded route. I haven't got a woman waiting for me so I've got more time than you. I'll take the same route in half an hour's time. Go on.'

'Where will you wait?'

'At the opening of the wood. Hurry up and go, will you.'

Ethelred suddenly felt a twinge of anxiety about Sally's illness. She had been delirious when he left the shed to meet Jack. He turned his back on him and started to walk through the wood, suddenly terrified that he would get back to the shed and find Sally dead.

'Ethelred,' called Jack.

'Yes?'

'When you get home, you won't find Sally dead. I can promise you that.'

Ethelred bitterly regretted not having a flask of gin in his pocket. He hurriedly opened the door of the shed. Sally was lying on her back, no longer delirious, her health almost restored.

'What time is it, Ethelred? Why have you left me alone for so long? You knew I was ill. It wasn't very gentlemanly of you.'

Ethelred sat down on the floor and took her hand in his.

'I had no choice, Sally. It was Jack. I had to help him. He was at the tavern in a dreadful state because of the death of his wife and child. His grief was worse than I've ever seen it. He told me he was going to end his life and I had to stop him. I gave him a whole bottle of gin to raise his spirits. Then I

141

walked him home and helped him into bed and waited for him to go to sleep.

'He must have pretended to be asleep. I left the room to get him some water in case he woke up thirsty. While I was out, he left the room and went to Priscilla's room where he took some arsenic from a chest on the table. He swallowed it and came back to his own room, leaving the empty bottle on the floor.

'When I came back with the water, I knew what he'd done. I had to go and wake up Mrs Dodderidge who brought a beaker of salt water. We forced Jack to swallow it and turned him onto his stomach with his head over the side of the bed. We got him to be sick.

'He realised the stupidity of his action and assured me he wouldn't do the same thing again, so I left him with Mrs Dodderidge to sit up with him.'

Whenever Ethelred lied, he was under the misguided impression that his listener would automatically believe him if he gave a complicated and interminable account of his version of the truth.

Even Sally, who was not overtly intelligent, failed to believe his extraordinary and complex story.

She said nothing and he was convinced she believed him although he was vexed by her failure to express sympathy. She closed her eyes, removed her hand from his and turned over, facing away from him.

Ethelred felt responsible for Sally and was attracted by her pertness, moodiness and petulance, combined with her skeletal hands and arms and her waif-like vulnerability. He enjoyed lying down beside her and having physical contact with her, even though carnal activity between them had stopped for a long time.

He liked being protective towards her because doing so asserted his masculinity and his gentleness and tenderness gave him the kudos of the strong tending the weak.

Despite his love for Sally, who reminded him of some of Malcolm Robertson's tiny birds, Ethelred felt more comfortable, stimulated and relaxed in Jack's company, and doted on his brother's protectiveness of him, in the same way he assumed Sally doted on his own protectiveness.

* * *

Two months passed. Jack was back playing at The Fife and Drum after visiting the other taverns, not because music comforted him any more, but because he knew that if he did not work he would go mad. Even after the passage of two months, there were not even remote signs that his grief was beginning to lessen and the only thing which comforted him was Ethelred's presence at meals. Although he reprimanded his brother every time he mimicked the eccentric, alcohol-dominated Mrs Dodderidge, secretly he basked in the humour and merriment he evoked, as the ability to laugh acted as a caressing elixir for his broken heart.

One morning when Ethelred met him for breakfast, instead of looking grief-stricken, he looked frightened and worried. He was unable to eat the steaming eggs Mrs Dodderidge had prepared for him.

'You look worried, Jack.'

'I am worried, I am worried about you.'

'Why?'

'I want you to come to live with me in this house.'

'I hate this house. I am very happy living with Sally. Besides, she needs me.'

Jack pushed his food from one side of the plate to the other, and then pushed it back again.

'I too need you,' he said furiously. 'I know you hate this house but you'll get used to it. I can't tolerate your living with Sally.'

Ethelred considered his brother's words intrusive and was irritated.

'You only say these things, Jack, because you are jealous of the fact that I have a woman waiting for me at home and you do not. I love Sally and she loves me and my love for her is such that I am seriously thinking of proposing marriage to her.'

'Don't expect me to attend the wedding,' said Jack.

'I won't. You won't be invited. You've no business making these dreadful demands and trying to interfere with my woman. Find yourself another woman of your own.'

Although Ethelred had only eaten half his food, his hunger had died. He pushed his chair away from the table and rose to his feet.

'I won't be having any more meals with you for the time being, Jack. I will see you when we work in the evenings but that will be all. It's time you learnt to eat on your own.'

He walked to the door and opened it and bumped into Mrs Dodderidge who was carrying a pot of steaming tea. She was startled and dropped the tea onto the floor. Ethelred had a nervous, giggling fit, made worse by his distress after quarrelling with the brother he worshipped.

'Are you all right, Mrs Dodderidge?' called Jack. 'I'll come out and help you pick up the broken china.'

Ethelred stood over Jack as he picked up the pieces. He felt both enraged and guilty, the guilt caused by the fact that he had refused to keep his brother company when he needed him most to alleviate his loneliness. He laid his hand on Jack's shoulder.

'Jack?'

Jack raised his head and looked him in the eye. Ethelred knew the look well. It was the look he gave to his victims before killing them.

'Goodbye, Ethelred,' he said.

'Goodbye, Jack. I wish we hadn't quarrelled.'

144

Ethelred could think of nothing further to say. He went into the hall, put on his coat and left through the front door to face the blinding rain. He felt very sad and hoped to find Sally at home to cheer him up.

Sally was there, cleaning the floor.

'You've made good timing, Ethie. I was just about to get tea ready. Take that wet coat off, or you'll catch a chill.'

Ethelred sat down. There were tears in his eyes.

'You're upset, Ethie. What's up?'

'Nothing. I just had a bit of an argument with Jack, that's all.'

'Don't worry, Ethie. I know you'll soon make it up.'

It was not long before the McArandys were having meals together again. Jack did not mention Sally, who continued to be consistently kind to Ethelred, in contrast with her cruel behaviour before he had thrown her out. She made what appeared to be a superhuman effort to make him comfortable and happy. She shaved him, brushed his hair, washed his clothes and even massaged his back and shoulders after cooking him appetising dinners when he returned late at night from the taverns.

'I've a surprise for you this evening, Ethie,' she said one evening, holding his hands as he came through the door.

'What's that, my girl?'

'I've made you your favourite pie tonight. Onions and cheese. You've often told me that's your favourite.'

* * *

Three years passed. Jack had almost recovered from his grief. He became closer to Ethelred and, as is the case with some men, Ethelred loved his brother more than his mistress. For a few years they lived in complete contentment. Jack and Sally became friends. She was a frequent and appreciative

145

guest at his house and, because of Jack's financial donations to his brother, she was always elegantly and decoratively dressed. She also managed to shed part of her Spitalfields street accent and adopt the more educated brogue which the McArandys' mother had taught them to speak with.

The happiness of the brothers did not last indefinitely. Ethelred's unhappiness developed gradually. There were times when he came home and found that Sally was no longer waiting for him. He had no idea where she was, but it did not take him long to realise that she was back on the streets.

At first, she was away for only two nights a week. Gradually, she increased her absences to three, four and sometimes five nights, but Ethelred's love for her was such that he refused to question her and behaved as if he accepted her absences. He continued to be loving and doting towards her but wept within and said nothing about it to Jack. When the brothers were together he pretended to be happy, with the skill that a professional actor might have envied, and even Jack, with his telepathic powers of reading his brother's mind, remained deceived.

One night Ethelred could contain his wretchedness no longer. When he tried to embrace Sally, she brushed him aside. The once hardened highwayman, crook and murderer burst into tears.

'Please tell me, Sally. This has been going on for so long now – your coldness, your unfriendliness, your absences. Is it something I've done? If it is, tell me and I will put it right.'

For the first time for some years, her green eyes were flooded with the evil glint that had made Ethelred shudder and Jack smoulder.

'Yes, Ethelred. It is something you've done. I should say something you did. I have not forgotten that time many years ago when you brutalised me and my lover, Christopher Ridgard, and I can tell you he is one hundred times the lover you was or ever could be.

146

'I can't forget the way you dragged him off me and threw us and my poor sister into the street to starve, like the villain and tyrant you are, underneath your repulsive, sham sweetness.

'Time does not lessen the wrong a person does. You and your stinking brother, Jack, are both evil and vile. The whole of London knows that, even though they bow down to you and cover up for you because, just by chance, you happen to give pleasure as musicians.'

Ethelred's normally robust skin went a pale shade of grey. He thought he was going to be sick.

'But Sally, we've been like husband and wife since then. We made it up!' he spluttered.

Sally walked backwards and forwards across the room, sweeping things off the table as she did so. She went up to Ethelred and stood so close to him that their faces were almost touching, while she spat further vitriol at him.

'You worthless fool! I only pretended to make it up. I forced myself to crawl back to you, and I can tell you that it felt as if the skin was being ripped from my knees.'

'Why did you crawl back to me? Why? Why? Why?'

'I'll tell you why, you murderer. I crawled back to you to trick you into loving me. Revenge to me is sweeter than life, sweeter than the air I breathed when I went away from London once. I've wanted it more than opium. I've been waiting patiently all this time, to allow your filthy love to build up, just so that I can hurt you more.'

Ethelred sat down at the table and ran his hands through his hair.

'You're mad, Sally. You're insane. You can't behave like this just because I lost my temper all those years ago. You're warped. You're distorted.'

'Just wait a minute, Ethelred. There's something I haven't told you yet. I've waited until this moment, and I've thought of nothing else, even when I pretended to love you and was nice to you.'

'What haven't you told me?'

'Because of my hatred of your simpering charm and your vile brother's brutality and the way he rapes and maims us whores. Because of what you did to us that day, Christopher Ridgard and I decided to do something to the pair of you, something that would break your rotten hearts of stone.'

Ethelred suddenly thought of his mother's murder and that of Benjamin Stern, whom he found dead on the floor, knifed in the back. The thought flashed through his mind that Sally couldn't conceivably have had any connection with that incident. For a moment, he was curious rather than mortified with mental pain.

'You'd better tell me what you did, Sally. Whatever it was, I want the subject over and done with. I've been working very hard. I'm upset, wretched and tired. Let's have it. What did you and Ridgard do?'

Sally sat down opposite Ethelred and folded her arms on the table. She was shaking with excitement and vindictive rage. Her eyes looked more evil than Ethelred had ever seen them. She let out a chilling, surreal laugh.

'I'll tell you what we did, Ethelred,' she said. 'We found out where your family lived. We was surprised it was so near here. We watched your cottage for some time. We found out your mother was ill. Someone in The Fife and Drum told us. We saw a man come into the cottage one night and we saw you and your brother leave. We knew what was up. You and your brother asked that man to look after your sick mother while you was both away.

'We waited for you to leave. We didn't think the man was suspecting attackers. Christopher threw his weight against the door. We went straight in. We saw your mother lying in bed on her back. We could tell she was in a lot of pain.

'The man, whoever he was, was standing nearby. We smiled at him, said "Good evening, sir," and asked if there was anything we could get for your mother. We said we was neighbours and had heard she was ill. The man said "Thank you" and that he could manage.

'Then for some reason he turned away from us. I don't know why, to this day. Christopher had a carving knife hidden under his coat. He rammed it into the man as hard as he could. It was all very sudden. The man fell dead.

'We had to get him out of the way because the person we really wanted to get at was your mother. We knew she was the dearest thing in the world to both of you and we had to make sure there was no one there to protect her.

'And now, Ethelred, here comes the best part. It wasn't Christopher who killed your mother. It was me. I shan't forget it to this day, Ethelred. Oh, how meadow-sweet it felt! I went straight for her eyes, Ethelred. There's something like that in one of them plays by Shakespeare, Christopher said, but I don't know none of his plays, being an uneducated whore.'

Ethelred was already green with horror.

'It … was *King Lear*,' he spluttered.

'The shock killed her, Ethelred. Christopher's more squeamish than me. He turned her body over onto her front.

'Do you know what, Ethelred? I had a burning urge to leave my mark by the man's dead body. The floor was dusty. I put my finger into the dust. I meant to write the words "GREEN EYES", but we heard someone walking past. I got scared. I only managed to write the letters GR.'

Sally stretched her arms, pulled up her dress and put her feet on the table. She smiled like a satiated cat.

'So that's about it, Ethelred. That's what happened. I'm glad I told you. I never thought it, but now that I've told you, I don't feel such hatred towards you any more.'

Ethelred sat motionless. He came out in a sweat and started to shake violently as if suffering from epilepsy. He couldn't speak. He couldn't even scream. He remained in this state for ten minutes. Then he leant forward and was sick.

There was one thing that Sally's hardened psyche could not tolerate and that was the sight of vomit. She hurriedly left the shed, heading for the streets.

Ethelred stayed seated for two hours. Then he staggered to a cupboard and drank half a bottle of gin, his mind busy. He knew he couldn't possibly approach Jack and tell him the story to his face. He also knew he couldn't go on living because he had betrayed Jack with his frailty. He knew Jack would have behaved differently on hearing Sally's gruesome confession.

He opened the table drawer and got out pen, paper and ink. He made a point of sitting at the end of the table, as far away as possible from where he had been sick.

He waited for his hand to become steadier before he began to write Sally's story in the form of a letter addressed to 'Jack, my brother and only friend.' The letter ended with the words, 'I betrayed you with my gutlessness, cowardice and weakness over a woman, my dearest Jack. Therefore, I must die.'

He left the letter on the table and went to the corner of the room where there was a protruding beam supporting the ceiling. He picked up a chair and carried it to the corner and stood on it. He removed his scarf and looped one end of it round the beam and adjusted the other end round his neck. Just before he kicked the chair from underneath him, he enjoyed a brief, pleasant memory of the games he and Jack had played in the cobbled street outside the cottage as children.

* * *

It was Jack who came into the shed and found Ethelred's body hanging from the beam. Ethelred had not turned up for work at the taverns, or visited the house for three days. Jack's initial reaction was to assume he had a fever, but he became suspicious because neither Sally, nor anyone else for that matter, had given him a message accounting for his brother's absence.

Regardless of his telepathic power, Jack knew nothing about the development of the dreadful relationship between Ethelred and Sally. He approached the shed with discretion in case the pair were being carnally active. He knocked delicately on the door and was surprised to get no answer. He waited for an hour. Then he asked a neighbour if he had seen his brother. The neighbour replied that Ethelred had not emerged from the shed for several days.

Jack heaved his weight against the door and on finding his brother's body, he acted with extraordinary alacrity for someone in severe shock. He picked up the chair which had been kicked on its side, stood on it and disentangled the scarf before lifting Ethelred to the floor.

He wept like a child, and cradled the body in his arms, muttering, 'My dear little brother, my poor little brother.'

He found the letter on the table and made a swift decision, firstly to savagely torture Sally and then to kill her. For this purpose, he would have to wait in the shed, assuming Sally would be returning soon as she would need somewhere to sleep. So that there would be no chance at all of her escaping on recognising him, he knew that he would have to disguise himself as Ethelred by painting a yellow streak next to his hairline.

He did this straight away by sprinkling some mustard powder from the cooking area, onto his hair and dabbing water onto it so that it would stay in place.

He concluded that Sally was not yet aware that Ethelred was dead, unless she had returned to the shed, panicked and run off.

He bundled Ethelred's body into a sack which he had found to be full of flour. He emptied the flour over the bushes at the back of the shed. Once the body was in the sack, he dragged it outside where he had poured the flour and managed to hide it among the bushes.

He then returned to the shed and drank some of the gin his brother had left.

He waited in the shed for two days, living on what to him was a repulsive diet of salami and raw cabbages. He stayed where he was as he had nothing to live for. He longed to be arrested and hanged. He was determined to wait until Sally returned so that he could murder her.

On the second night, he kept himself awake for as long as he could. At 2.00 a.m., he fell asleep with his head on the table, with the blond streak visible.

It was not until 3.30 a.m. that he was jolted from sleep by the sound of the door opening. Sally came in, dishevelled, drunk and singing tunelessly.

Jack looked her in the face and smiled. He had no idea how Ethelred had related to women in private, so he said as little as possible, mimicking his brother's voice which was slightly less refined than his own.

'You were out very late tonight,' he said quietly. 'I was wondering if you were all right.'

She said nothing. She staggered over to the mattress and lay down without removing her clothes.

Jack was nauseated by her sluttishness, and although sick with grief, he was partly angry with his brother because of his tastes in women.

Sally lay on her back with her eyes open and her legs parted through habit.

'Well, Ethelred. I'm still awake, you know. Do you think you'll be able to manage? You've done nothing like this for years.'

Jack had had no idea that Ethelred had sometimes suffered from impotence and prolonged lack of sexual activity, as he hadn't really understood what his brother was referring to when he had once mentioned his difficulties with women.

It was Sally's question that made him decide to cause her as painful a death as possible there and then.

He went over to the table drawer and took out a carving knife, which he brought over to the mattress where Sally lay with her eyes closed.

'Didn't you hear me, Ethelred, you deaf fool?' she said.

Jack gave her a thunderous slap across the face. Had she been less drunk she would have been astounded by Ethelred's gesture which was entirely out of character.

'Yes, I heard you,' said Jack. 'There's something else you ought to know.'

'What? I'm so confused. You've never hit me before.'

'Ethelred's dead, you stinking whore! You drove him to suicide. He hanged himself. You thought I was Ethelred, didn't you? I am not Ethelred. I'm Jack.'

Sally looked aghast, even in her drunkenness.

'The moon is full,' said Jack. 'That's when madmen commit murder. You can see the blond streak in my hair, can't you? That's why you thought I was Ethelred.'

He guided her hand to the congealed mustard and water in his hair. Its stiffness brought her to her senses. She knew then that the man was definitely Jack.

'Do you remember when you asked me to play *Where Have You Been, Lord Rendal, My Son?*'

'Yes, Jack!'

'It's your favourite, isn't it?'

'Yes, Jack!'

'Then I will sing it for you, and while I am singing it, I am going to kill you. Between each line or so, I will tell you exactly how I am going to kill you.'

'All right, Jack,' was all Sally could think of saying.

Jack lowered his voice to a hoarse whisper.

'I'm going to begin now. As you can see, I am holding a carving knife.'

153

He waved the knife in the air in rhythm with his beautiful singing.

'Where have you been, Lord Rendal, my son?'

'Now, I'm going to slit you from navel to breastbone.'
Jack did what he said he was going to do but miraculously, Sally remained alive.

'Where have you been, my handsome young one?
I'm going to the green wood, Mother, make my bed soon.'

'Now, I'm going to hack out your stinking liver!'

'For I am very sick and I fain would lie down.'

Sally was already dead. Jack rose to his feet and briefly looked at her savagely-mutilated body, illuminated by the moon. Then he laughed for an hour like a demented maniac until he finally fell asleep on the floor, exhausted.

He was still asleep at 6.00 a.m. He was not woken by the door being opened silently by Sally's sister, Meg Parry, who had spent the night with a wealthy private tutor to some rich children, and earned three times as much as the wage to which she was accustomed.

Meg had only opened the door two inches before she saw her sister's mutilated body on the mattress and the sleeping body of Jack McArandy lying curled in a foetal position on the floor. She closed the door quietly behind her and rushed out to get help.

Jack's extensive career as a criminal had, until then, been facilitated by the lack of an efficiently organised police force. He was fortunate that he did not live 100 years after his time.

The least inactive enforcer of a semblance of law and order was known as the Parish Constable, supervised in theory by the High Constable. Both were part of a body of 'overseers', including church wardens and alleged surveyors of London roads.

The latter category might just as well have been dormant, due to permanently loose cobblestones and holes in the roads, deep enough to rock carriages, and in some cases even to topple them over. Added to these problems, breakdowns in communications between members of law-enforcing bodies were frequent.

The duties of a Parish Constable were not made easier by the poorly-lit streets or the fact that he and his colleagues were outnumbered by criminals, by the darkness befriended. His task was made difficult by the narrow London alleys and the existence in some places of a network of underground, warren-like tunnels, where felons could hide and escape from one area to another.

Law-breakers like the McArandys and their network of friends and accomplices were often armed with pistols, bludgeons, cutlasses and other such lethal weapons. Even during daylight hours, the law-abiding feared travelling in carriages in the rougher area of Spitalfields and those who summoned the courage to venture onto the streets, felt as if they were crossing a cannon-laden battlefield.

Among his arduous and psychologically taxing duties, the Parish Constable's task was to raise the hue and cry in the all-too prevalent events of violence towards the frail, pilfering, robbery, rape and murder. Were it not for the primitive structure of law-enforcing bodies, to which his stressful services contributed, the McArandys would have been caught when they had committed their first joint crime of murdering their father and swinging his body into the Thames.

Punishments for the criminals, who were actually caught, were severe, but because professional criminals were rarely caught, risks were recklessly taken and crime remained rife.

For very minor offences, criminals unfortunate enough to be caught had their arms put into wooden stocks and were forced to go for long periods without food and drink. Sometimes, they were thrashed with a cat-o'-nine-tails or scorched by a branding iron. Often, they faced deportation or hanging, even for minor acts of theft.

* * *

Half an hour after Meg's escape from the shed, Jack woke to find the armed Parish Constable and two of his colleagues surrounding him as he lay on the floor. The Parish Constable, a short, stout, red-faced man, was foul-tempered because he loathed his occupation, which was difficult to replace. He grabbed Jack by the hair and wrenched him to his feet.

'Are you Ethelred McArandy?' he shouted.

'No. I am Jack McArandy. Ethelred is dead.'

'He was your brother, was he not?'

'Yes.'

'How did he die?'

'He committed suicide. The dead woman you see over there broke his heart. She also told him she had gouged out our mother's eyes when she was dying.'

The Parish Constable looked confused.

'When who was dying?'

'Our mother,' said McArandy, too tired and bleary-eyed to show emotion.

'Where did he do it?' asked the Parish Constable.

'Where did who do what?'

'Don't you dare pretend to be half-witted when speaking to me! Where did your brother commit suicide?'

'Over there in the corner.'

'Where is his body?'

'I put it in a sack behind the shed.'

'Why?'

McArandy was still too shocked and exhausted to gather his wits.

'Why did he kill himself over there in the corner or why did I put his body in a sack?' he asked.

The Parish Constable had had enough of his work, his misery and his life. He hit McArandy, knocking him down, and kicked him in the stomach, before pulling him to his feet.

'Why did you put your brother's body into a sack? If he killed himself, what had you to hide?'

'I hid him so that I could disguise myself as Ethelred by putting a blond streak in my hair. I did that so that Sally over there would think I was Ethelred and make it easier for me to kill her. Otherwise, she might have escaped. She was an evil, criminal woman, considering she did such a thing to our mother. I was only taking justice into my own hands to relieve the likes of you of some of your responsibilities.'

'Don't try to be flippant a second time, McArandy, or you'll be sorry,' said the Parish Constable. 'Where did your mother live?'

'In a cottage two streets away. There was a man looking after her when we were away called Benjamin Stern. He was stabbed in the back by a man called Christopher Ridgard, Sally's fancy fellow. Then Sally gouged out our mother's eyes.'

'You will accompany us to the cottage, McArandy,' said the Parish Constable.

'We have a problem here,' said McArandy. 'We burnt it down.'

'Why?'

McArandy feigned tears.

'We'd been robbed in the street. We didn't have enough money to pay for our friend to be buried, and our mother to have a funeral fitting to our proud McArandy blood.'

'Folks like you don't appear to have much blood to be proud of,' said the Parish Constable.

'Our mother never committed a crime in her life. I take your remark as an insult. All she did was wash, cook and clean and supplement our income by taking in work as a seamstress. Perhaps you think you have reason to consider me to be a bit of a bounder but, no matter who you are, I'll fight you with fisticuffs if you dare even think of saying anything untoward about Ethelred's and my mother.'

The Parish Constable thought he was being lashed across the face with a wet towel. He grabbed McArandy by the arms.

'Did I hear you use the word "bounder"?' he bellowed. 'Bounder? Bounder? Are you telling me that that mutilated woman with her entrails seeping half way across the floor was killed by a mere bounder?'

McArandy knew he was finished and decided to use black humour to lessen his despair.

'All right, all right. I know I'm for the gallows, but because of my extraordinary honesty, I do think I deserve to be hanged with a silken cord like a peer of the realm.'

Strangely, the Parish Constable did actually have a sense of humour and although he hadn't shown it earlier, Jack's responses to his questions made it hard for him and his colleagues to keep a straight face.

'Some years ago, you and your brother committed an act of highway robbery in Hertfordshire, didn't you?' said the Parish Constable.

'No,' said McArandy, 'I've never been to Hertfordshire. I hadn't even heard of the place until now.'

'A coachman described your appearances. He saw you ride through the fields on a single horse, after you murdered a lady and gentleman travelling in the carriage.'

'That incident never occurred and whoever told you it did is a confounded liar. If it did, why did you not arrest my brother and me earlier?'

The Parish Constable evaded the question.

'Is the name George Robertson familiar to you?'

'No. I've never heard of him.'

'His neighbours saw you and your brother drag him away from the street he lived in. His body was found floating in the Thames.'

'Oh, was it?'

'Did you know a Henry Talbot of Tinley Street?'

'No.'

'His body was found in his bed. He had been bludgeoned to death.'

'That may well be, but it had nothing to do with me.'

'Only one night later the body of an old gentleman by the name of Malcolm Robertson was found under his bed, covered by a blanket.'

'I don't know anything about that either.'

In view of the fact that Jack had been caught red-handed, after Sally's murder, the Parish Constable was swift to arrest him. It was now only a matter of time before his trial and hanging at Tyburn, where he would get the vast audience for which he yearned.

Now that Ethelred and Priscilla were dead, McArandy no longer wished to live so he made the most of his fantasies and delusions of grandeur. Each night he dreamed of the day when he would be driven through the streets of London, his ultimate destination being the scaffold, which would bring him the sweetness of death, for which he had craved like a beautiful, perfumed woman.

* * *

Jack McArandy was hanged on a warm June dawn beneath a cloudless, *vin rosé* sky.

When the cart carrying him arrived at the Tyburn execution field the multitude of spectators who had gathered, fuelled his euphoria. His mother, Priscilla, and Ethelred had all met violent deaths and the anticipation that he would be following them in a matter of minutes, filled his soul with a joy that had been equalled only when he had been told he was to become a father.

The horse and cart driven by the hangman, came to a halt under Tyburn Tree where the gallows had been built to hang 21 prisoners at once. Because he was such a notorious, as well as popular prisoner, McArandy was to be hanged alone and the notion of having the whole gallows to himself boosted his vanity and added to his sense of well-being.

He looked about him and noticed that the grandstand seats were occupied by the myriad of people he had played to regularly while doing the rounds of the taverns. Two thirds of these spectators were his loyalest and most devoted friends and fellow felons. They had been enraptured by his and Ethelred's musicianship.

Many of the grandstand spectators, both men and women alike, had either saved or stolen to afford their seats. They wept openly and clapped and cheered as the horse and cart stopped under Tyburn Tree. Even the hangman, a sympathetic, but verbose man called Ned Robson, had regularly attended recitals by the McArandys and although he had only rarely spoken to them, the task ahead of him broke his heart and he, too, wept openly.

Apart from the spectators, who had queued for ten days to watch the hanging, the other onlookers, whose throng stretched as far as the horizon, had little knowledge of the good side of the McArandys and had gathered in a spirit of callous, ghoulish hatred. But to McArandy, their jeers and shouts of abuse seemed outweighed by the cheers of his supporters.

Ned Robson, the hangman, discreetly turned to McArandy and winked at him. The mere act of winking caused another tear to stray down his cheek. McArandy knew what Robson intended to say, namely that he would give him as much time as he needed to speak to his supporters and even grant them a musical request, before blindfolding him and tying his hands and lashing the horse's reins that would wing his soul to eternity.

As McArandy watched his supporters, they sang a ditty to a tune similar to *Clementine*, '*McArandy, do not leave us. McArandy, do not die.*' McArandy waited for the singing to die down before he addressed them in a powerful, resonant voice:

'Ladies and gentlemen, my dear brothers and sisters, I am moved beyond words, by your coming here, just to say "farewell" to a humble, felonious musician.

'Of the thousands standing like a dense forest before me, I know which of you are for me and which are agin me. Those of you agin me do not know me, but there is nothing a McArandy loves more than an audience, so I thank you all the same.

'Now, a word to those dear friends who are for me. I do not see this lofty gibbet as a fearsome thing. Its very wood is that of a sailing vessel to carry me home to my loved ones, my mother, Ethelred, my brother and Priscilla, my lady love who shared my life and, but for an illness, would have been the mother of my son stillborn.

'I have no wish to rob the sweet and maternal scaffold of its prey. I welcome death. I have no fear of it, so I want you all to dry your tears. Instead, you should be rejoicing for my happiness.'

Apart from the crowd of McArandy supporters, their eyes reddened with grief, there was an atmosphere of *bonhomie* and camaraderie among the vast crowd, not dissimilar to that of a country fête.

Stalls sold miniature gibbets, hanging dolls which were identical models of McArandy. Even they did not distort the deceptively beautiful features of a man who had committed so many crimes. Each doll intricately showed his thick, wavy, black hair and almond-shaped, dark eyes.

The crowd consisted of the rich, the reasonably well-off, the poor and even children. Among these were people who despised McArandy, while some of them, though antagonistic towards him, somehow regarded him as an evil, but endearing anti-hero.

When McArandy noticed the hostile expressions on the faces of some of these spectators, he felt challenged and stimulated, for he liked his audiences to show a mixture of hatred and adulation. As he looked at the gibbet, slightly obscured by the rising June sun, he likened the simple, wooden structure to Priscilla's beckoning arms after she had laid down her needlework.

To him, it represented a vehicle taking him to her soft, white flesh and her joyously opening legs in readiness to receive his seed. He saw the noose not far above his head as a magical entity which would entwine her graceful and divine soul with his own for eternity.

He smiled at his supporters and the rest of the crowd and when many waved and smiled back, he could see Priscilla's bright, even-toothed smile on each of their faces.

He turned to the occupants of the grandstand.

'Ladies and gentlemen, brothers and sisters, have you any last request before my soul is united with my loved ones?'

The occupants of the grandstand were unanimous, and repeatedly chanted '*Lord Rendal*' until they reached a frenzied climax of hysteria.

McArandy turned to Robson, the hangman, and caught his eye. Robson smiled back to suggest that he was prepared to give him more time, before covering his eyes with a black cloth and binding his hands.

'Sing first, sir. Then I'll have to tie and blindfold you and be off with the horse.'

The hangman was unable to look him in the eye. His voice was hushed and shaky with emotion. He told himself he would abandon his career and seek another trade. He felt tarnished and sullied like a cold-blooded murderer, since there was neither passion nor malice in him towards the beautiful-looking musician whom he had been ordered to kill.

He said, 'I am sorry but I will have to blindfold you now, sir and tie your hands behind your back. It breaks my heart but I have no choice.'

'It's not your fault, my friend. Could you allow me to grant these people's request first?'

The hangman knew that Jack McArandy would be the last man he ever hanged, so he had no fear of being disciplined by his superiors, since he had decided to abandon his trade.

'God bless you, sir,' he said, 'I'd rather burn in hell than deny these people their pleasure. I want you to meet your God singing to him, not cowering before him with your head bowed in shame.'

'I will meet no God but I will be united with those I love.'

The chanting of 'Lord Rendal' continued and grew louder and louder. Suddenly, a twelve-year-old beggar-boy among the crowd close to the gibbet forced his way forward. He was dirty, undernourished and sparsely covered with pitiful rags. His face had not been washed for some weeks which gave him a negroid look. From his blackened face, two big blue eyes beamed.

The people in the crowd were staggered by the fact that the ragged, urchin-like boy was carrying a lute, for he was a musician. He ran to the condemned man's cart and because he was too shy to hand the lute to McArandy, he thrust it into the hands of the flabbergasted hangman.

His accent was rough and hard to understand.

He shouted, 'You always was my hero, Mr McArandy, sir! Use my lute and sing your song.'

McArandy nearly burst into tears but controlled himself. The hangman handed him the lute.

'Sing first, sir,' he said. 'Then I'll have to do my sad duty.'

McArandy sang *Lord Rendal* with a voice of such unparalled beauty that those in earshot of him felt as if hot nectar were being poured into their ears, before swimming round their heads and soaking into their brains. They felt hot, silvery gin trickling down their throats and into their stomachs, before coursing through their veins. They jumped up and down, screaming and cheering. Although they knew they were about to lose McArandy they felt a surge of almost sexual joy.

As he listened to the song the beggar-boy stood by the cart and ran his hands along its edge, as it was carrying his hero. When McArandy had finished singing, he bent over and passed the lute back to the boy.

'Sweet little lad!' he muttered, pressing his mouth to the boy's ear. 'No one in this crowd will forget you. It is you, little one, and not I, who are a hero.'

The boy looked as if he had received a papal blessing. His dirty cheeks were flushed with pride. He carried his lute like a baby that had just been christened and immersed himself in the crowd, while some of the people stroked his head and patted him on the back. He could not bear to witness the hanging and covered his eyes.

In contrast to the song, a priest sombrely recited prayers: '*May the peace of God which passeth all understanding ...*'.

His prayer was accompanied by a dramatic roll of drums and a high-pitched bleating of pipes. The hangman, his face sodden with tears, blindfolded McArandy and bound his hands. McArandy suddenly began to feel tired, bored and irritated.

The hangman took the horse's reins and turned to face him.

'I won't ever be hanging anyone else after this, sir. How can I do a duty which destroys my soul and makes my heart bleed? You're a fine, grand lion of a fellow and I'd shake your hand if it wasn't tied behind your back. I'm afraid I'll be off with the horse now. Farewell, Jack McArandy.'

164

McArandy thought the hangman had become annoyingly over-talkative. He would have appreciated the opportunity to spend the last few seconds of his life in contemplative silence. He recognised the hangman's tedious display of emotion, combined with the fact that he had a kind heart.

He was sufficiently considerate towards him, not to let him grieve too much after his death, and decided to be abrupt with him, partly because his last thoughts had been intrusively interrupted and partly because he didn't want the hangman to miss him and suffer the symptoms of bereavement. He changed his tone from endearing, humane platitudes, and his voice took on a clipped, savage rasp.

'Damn you, man, you talk far too much! What dying man can possibly tolerate your eternal, back-baiting prattle? Do you usually make interminable, unwarranted speeches to luckless bastards who have got to swing?'

The hangman was stunned by McArandy's sudden outburst of irritability, contrasting confusingly with his formerly affable behaviour. Because he was so astounded he pulled tightly on the horse's reins, making it run backwards, causing the cart to hit the first two steps leading to the gallows. The occupants of the grandstand witnessed the tragic indignity of the episode and broke into hysterical giggles, combined with sobbing. The hangman was mortified with embarrassment and shame.

'Go not to your God in a bad temper, sir,' he spluttered.

'There is no God, you fool! I was enjoying this at the beginning. Now, I feel exhausted, low-spirited and dejected. Control your horse and get me away from this sickening, vile life!'

The hangman whitened. He was an even-tempered man who was unable to understand mood swings in others. For a moment he thought he was going to faint but the feeling passed. As he lashed the reins that would carry his strange prisoner's soul into eternity, he tremulously muttered the word 'farewell' a second time, unhappy and confused by his partially hostile feelings towards a man he felt he actually loved.

McArandy died instantly. His many friends rushed to his body and released it by its legs and beat the stomach area and chest to make sure he was dead and no longer suffering. Some of his more superstitious friends touched the body in the hope that it might have medicinal qualities and others did so in the misguided hope that the body might pass on the gift of musicianship.

An infatuated woman, who had always listened to the McArandys at The Fife and Drum, had been too shy to introduce herself to them. To make up for it she bared one of her breasts, and guided McArandy's lifeless hand to it, fanatically rubbing the hand against it and letting out a hysterical wail.

Robson felt wretched. He returned to the gibbet and cut off a yard of the rope which had hanged his prisoner, rolled it up and put it in his pocket.

As was customary among hangmen, he travelled to an alehouse in Fleet Street, where rope which had hanged a man was sold at sixpence an inch. He hated having to do this and only did so to help settle his mounting drinking debts. He drank four tankards of ale to drown his misery as well as his shame through having been mercenary at McArandy's expense.

* * *

When Sally's sister, Meg Parry, attended the hanging, she was accompanied by her close friend, Liz who worked on the same beat as her at Spitalfields and who had also been a close friend of her murdered sister.

Like many prostitutes, Meg and Liz were lesbians and shared in common a fascination for public executions and

166

the sexual sensations they inspired in certain women, particularly when they drank gin from a stone bottle as the noose tightened round the prisoner's neck.

As the hangman drove the horse and cart away, the two women kissed on the mouth, running their hands through each other's tangled hair. They then returned to the tiny, squalid room they shared in Spitalfields. They hurriedly removed their clothes and rolled about on the floor, indulging in urgent, bizarre frolics before resorting to gentle caresses.

On the outside of the execution field, a rich family had gathered, consisting of an indulgent mother and four little girls, whose ages ranged from six to ten. Their mother spoilt them and only agreed to take them to Tyburn because they nagged her persistently and she was keener on a quiet life than on arguments with her little girls.

She was determined to remain on the outside of the field, in her carriage, as she did not want her daughters to see the hanging. She remained in the carriage most of the time, while the girls played on the damp, sweet-smelling grass nearby.

The children had on white cotton dresses and floral decorations in their hair. From the distance, they looked angelic but close up they looked mischievous and scheming. Because they had risen early that morning they had black circles under their small-pupilled blue eyes, which gave them a sinister appearance.

They formed a circle and held hands. Then they began to dance round and round, delightedly singing a song appropriate for the occasion.

> *McArandy was hanged on the gibbet high,*
> *Shortly after the deed was done.*
> *'Twas a desolate place at the back of a shed,*
> *A place for the timid to shun.*

McArandy will long be the banquet of crows
Which will flock on his carcass to batten.
The sumptuous morsels which fall from their beaks,
*The lank weeds beneath them will flatten.**

Even when the hanging was over the little girls were reluctant to leave the field. They ignored their mother's persistent pleas to come to her. In the end, she got out of her carriage and rounded them up. She put her long, thin, protective arms round all four of them.

'Do, please, get into the carriage, my darlings. I don't want you to be late for your French lesson.'

'But we couldn't even see the hanging from here, Mama,' said the oldest one. 'What was the point of getting up so early when we didn't see anything?'

The girls struggled from their mother's grip. The mother continued to call her children who became rowdier and more defiant. They were already exhausted by their early start, which made them bad-tempered and increasingly determined to disobey their mother. They smiled insolently at her and held hands, forming themselves into a circle once more. They sang another macabre ditty, this time out of tune, due to their tiredness, and repeated the couplet three times in order to get on their mother's nerves.

At the foot of the gibbet the mandrake springs,
Just where the creaking carcass swings.

As if to infuriate the mother, the oldest girl jumped up and down, shouting, 'We're staying here all day, Mama. Come and catch us if you can. We want to see the murdering man!'

*By courtesy of Harrison-Ainsworth (*Grimrod*). The author has taken the liberty of changing the tenses of some of the verbs, and altering certain words.

'I'm not staying here arguing,' said the mother impatiently. 'I'm not having you being late for your French lesson. If you don't get into the carriage immediately, Papa will smack you all when you get home. Come on, now. Hurry up.'

* * *

Meg Parry continued to flounce up and down the filthy Spitalfields street outside the rough, shabby tavern, from which the drunks were emerging. She caused a little party to gather, which increased in size until men and women began to dance drunkenly as if it were May Day. Meg lifted her stone gin bottle to her lips and became drunker and drunker. Her companions copied her until the party almost turned into a riot.

A burly, jovial-looking town-crier had to walk straight through the revellers who ignored him and continued to dance, densely occupying the width of the narrow, foul-smelling street. The town-crier was undeterred and went about his business, shouting, 'Eleven o'clock and all's well! McArandy was hanged on the gibbet high!'

The revellers, originally led by Meg, who had become so drunk that she lay sprawled in a doorway, cheered robustly on hearing the town-crier's words. Some of them repeated them, mimicking his voice. Popular though the McArandys had been, they were now hated in this part of Spitalfields, because of Meg's sister's savage murder.

The town-crier, though high-spirited, was becoming pleasantly tired but continued for a while:

'Twelve o'clock and all's well! McArandy was hanged on the gibbet high!'

He continued to repeat his words at hourly intervals until his throat was hoarse. When he became too exhausted and husky to cry out his message, he stopped, and his healthy, apple-cheeked face froze into a peaceful and contented smile.

169